Books in The Nancy Drew Files™ Series

Available from ARCHWAY Paperbacks

THE
NANCY DREW
FILES™

Case 56

MAKE NO MISTAKE

CAROLYN KEENE

AN ARCHWAY PAPERBACK
Published by POCKET BOOKS
New York   London   Toronto   Sydney   Tokyo   Singapore

AN ARCHWAY PAPERBACK *Original*

An Archway Paperback published by
POCKET BOOKS, a division of Simon & Schuster
1230 Avenue of the Americas, New York, NY 10020

ISBN: 0-671-70033-2

First Archway Paperback printing February 1991

10 9 8 7 6 5 4 3 2 1

Chapter
One

TALK ABOUT SLEAZY. Look at this headline," Bess Marvin said indignantly, sliding *Today's Times* across the kitchen table to Nancy Drew. "The poor guy's dead, and all anyone can talk about is his money."

Nancy pushed her reddish blond hair back from her face and looked up distractedly from the table, which was covered with the components of her car's tape deck. It kept eating her tapes, and she had taken it apart to see if she could fix it.

Picking up the newspaper, the slender eighteen-year-old glanced at the headline Bess had mentioned. It ran in big letters across the front page of the paper: "Glover's Millions Up for Grabs."

1

"It's pretty pathetic," she agreed after skimming the article. "That reporter was so busy writing about how big Mr. Glover's estate is that he hardly even mentioned his heart attack or any of the many donations Mr. Glover made to charities." She turned her attention back to the pile of components in front of her.

"I bet everyone in River Heights will be at his funeral tomorrow," said Bess, her blue eyes shining. "I mean, how often does a multimillionaire die without anyone to inherit his estate? His fortune's worth over ten million dollars!"

Nancy was fitting two tiny metal components together and pressing an even tinier metal spring between them. Without looking up, she said, "Oh, I'm sure there'll be somebody. A man with wings of hospitals named after him isn't going to forget to make a will. Now that I think of it, I remember my dad mentioned one."

Carson Drew, one of River Heights's most prominent lawyers, had been Clayton Glover's attorney. Nancy knew her father was involved with the settling of his estate, but she didn't know any of the details. "He'll probably leave most of his money to charity," she told Bess, "and a nice bit to Mrs. Adams."

"Oh, the housekeeper, that's right," said Bess. "Remember how great it was when we used to spend time out at Glover's Corners. You know, back when"—she paused uncertainly before finishing—"back when Matt was around."

Nancy and Bess had been in junior high when Matt Glover was reported missing in Colorado after an avalanche sent tons of snow tumbling into a mountain pass. He had been on a ski trip with four other boys in his freshman college class, Nancy remembered. Four bodies were discovered when the snows melted. Matt's was never found. It had made headlines in all the major newspapers in the area.

"I haven't thought about Matt much lately. I used to think about him all the time after he disappeared," Bess went on.

Something about the wistful note in Bess's voice made Nancy glance up to study her friend. There was a dreamy look in Bess's blue eyes, and she was twisting her long blond hair absently in her fingers. "Disappeared?" Nancy repeated. "You almost sound as if you think he could still be alive."

"I know there's no way he could be," Bess said slowly. "But for a while after he disappeared, I used to have this kind of fantasy—you know, where he would reappear, just like that, and we'd go back to skating and stuff out at the Corners. It was just wishful thinking, but I half convinced myself that he really *would* come back." She let out a little laugh. "I guess I have a pretty strong imagination."

Nancy smiled. "Well, it's understandable. Even though we were five or six years younger than Matt, he invited us all to skate and hang out at Glover's Corners. He was almost a hero to us."

"Almost? He *was* a hero, at least to me. Too bad it was only in my mind that he survived that avalanche." Bess sighed, resting her chin on her hands. After a short silence, she said, "Speaking of heroes, how's Ned?"

A familiar warm glow spread through Nancy at the mention of her longtime boyfriend, Ned Nickerson. Ned attended Emerson College, which was several hours' drive from River Heights.

"He's fine," Nancy answered. "He might make it home for a visit next weekend. I hope he can. Since I'm not on a case, I'd be able to spend lots of time with him."

Nancy's talent as a detective was well known in River Heights. She wasn't a professional, but people often asked for her help in solving mysteries. Sometimes it seemed that her detective work took up all her time, though. She was always grateful for free time to be with Ned and her friends.

Her stomach growled, and Nancy realized she was hungry. Giving up on her tape deck, she swept the components into a plastic bag, then went over to the kitchen cabinets.

"Want some popcorn?"

"Don't tempt me," Bess said, eyeing the jar Nancy pulled from the cabinet. "I'm trying to lose a few pounds."

Nancy smiled. Bess was *always* trying to lose a few pounds, even though she was the only one who thought she needed to. Her curvy figure— now covered with hot pink leggings and an oversize pink- and white-striped sweater—was different from Nancy's slender, taller build, but it suited Bess perfectly.

Nancy held the popcorn out temptingly, and Bess frowned. "Pretty sneaky plan, Nan, trying to distract me from thinking about Matt with popcorn."

"Is it working?"

"Well . . ." The frown was slowly replaced by a big grin. "You bet! I'll get the popper," she offered, going over to the cupboard. "Anyway, I read somewhere that popcorn has hardly any calories as long as you don't add butter."

Soon they had a heaping bowl of fluffy, butterless popcorn on the table between them. Bess reached for a big handful, popping the kernels one at a time into her mouth.

"I know it's morbid," she said, "but I keep thinking about how great it was when Matt was around and we used to go out to Glover's Corners."

Nancy nodded. "It was fun." In the winter, she remembered, there'd been ice skating on the pond behind the house. In the summer the pond was fringed with low-hanging willow trees, and Mrs. Adams, the housekeeper, would bring them ice-cold lemonade after they'd swum.

"Poor Mrs. Adams," Nancy said. "Now that Mr. Glover is gone, I wonder what she'll do."

Rosemary Adams had been more than just a housekeeper to the Glovers. Since Matt's mother had died when he was only ten, she'd been like a mother to him. It was hard to imagine Glover's Corners without her.

The girls looked up from their popcorn as Carson Drew came into the kitchen. Putting down his briefcase, he greeted Nancy and Bess, and Nancy saw at once that he was preoccupied. His forehead was creased, and his eyes were red looking.

"Hi, Mr. Drew," said Bess. She peered at her watch, then hopped up and began putting on her red down coat. "I guess I'd better go. It's almost time for dinner."

"I might as well tell you both right now," Carson said, not listening to Bess. "It's going to be all over town soon enough."

Both girls looked at him expectantly.

"I had a call from Rosemary Adams at Glover's Corners," he said. "A young man came to the door this afternoon." Carson hesitated, almost as if he couldn't continue with what he had to say.

"What did he want?" Nancy prompted.

"He said he was Matthew Glover, and Rosemary nearly fainted from the shock."

Nancy's mouth fell open. She started to say something, but her words were drowned out by Bess's excited cry.

"You see," she shouted, her face flushed pink. "I was right all along. Matt's alive, and he's come home!"

Chapter
Two

NANCY GLANCED from Bess's ecstatic face to Carson Drew's serious one. "Could it really *be* Matt?" she asked her father. "Is it possible?"

"Of course it's possible," Bess cut in impatiently.

"I haven't met him yet myself," Carson said, rubbing his eyes, "but Mrs. Adams swears that he looks and acts like Matt. But she's not sure he is Matt. Apparently, he says he had amnesia after his skiing accident. It wasn't until he saw Clayton Glover's picture in the paper that he remembered who he was." He shook his head and added, "As to whether or not he's telling the truth, I don't want to make any kind of judgment until I meet him."

"That's a good idea, Dad. And I think we

should do the same." Nancy stared meaningfully at Bess. "Right, Bess?"

"What? Oh—yeah, sure, Nan," Bess said, but the dreamy expression on her face told Nancy that her friend had already made up her mind.

"You were right, Bess," Nancy said in a low voice the following afternoon. "I think all of River Heights *is* here for Mr. Glover's funeral."

Nancy, Bess, and Bess's cousin George Fayne were entering the stone church where the service was to be held.

"It is really packed," George agreed. "I bet most of these people never even met Mr. Glover." Tall and slim, with short dark hair, George squeezed in next to Bess and Nancy in a pew toward the rear of the church.

Nancy peered toward the front of the church and found Rosemary Adams, dressed all in black. Nancy knew she must be in her sixties, but the silver-haired woman looked frailer than her years. Her face was dead white, and she was leaning heavily on Nancy's father's arm.

"Where is he?" Bess asked, craning her neck to scan the church.

Nancy didn't have to ask who "he" was. And from the amount of whispering Nancy heard, she guessed a lot of other people were wondering where Matt Glover was, too.

"Shh," said George. "The service is starting."

It wasn't until after the funeral that they got a

glimpse of Matt Glover. Many of the mourners lingered outside the church, and Nancy, George, and Bess paused, too.

Nancy was buttoning up her fleece-lined leather jacket when she heard Bess give a little shriek.

"There he is!" she exclaimed. "Wow, he's as great looking as ever!"

Nancy and George turned to follow Bess's gaze. Nancy spotted the tall, lanky guy at once. He was about twenty-three or -four, the age Matt would be, and he had the thick black hair and dark eyebrows Nancy remembered. He was approaching her father and Rosemary Adams, and Nancy saw his face light up with the wide grin that had been Matt's trademark.

"I'd die to have him look at me with that smile," Bess said with a sigh. "That's Matt, all right."

George rolled her eyes at her cousin. "That's your purely objective opinion, right?" she teased. Taking another look at the guy, she added, "I don't know. I don't remember Matt's shoulders being quite so broad."

"A man can change in five years," Bess said defensively. "He was our age when he died. When he disappeared, I mean," she corrected herself.

Privately, Nancy agreed with Bess. A lot of things about a person could change over time. Even so, this guy looked incredibly like the Matt she remembered. If he was an impostor, he was a very good one.

"They're coming over," Bess said excitedly.

A moment later the three girls were saying hello to Carson Drew and Mrs. Adams. They tried not to stare too openly at the young man with Carson as he introduced him.

"I'd like you to meet my daughter, Nancy," Carson said. "Nancy, this is"—he hesitated before saying it—"Matthew Glover."

Nancy knew her father didn't necessarily believe the stranger's identity, but what else could he call him? Nancy realized that she, too, had already started to think of him as Matt, even though she wasn't convinced he was the *real* Matt.

Whoever he was, his smile was easy and unforced. Up close Nancy could see that he had Matt's deep blue eyes and dark lashes. Bess was right about one thing—he *was* great looking!

"Nancy Drew," he said. "I knew you'd grow up to be beautiful."

For a second she thought he was trying to flirt with her. But then he smiled in a friendly, direct way. When Carson introduced him to Bess and George, he was just as charming with them.

"It's great to see you again," Bess told Matt. Nancy could almost see stars in Bess's eyes. "I always kept up a tiny hope that you'd come back."

"Thanks, Bess. That means a lot to me," Matt told her as he flashed her one of his big smiles.

Nancy had the distinct feeling that someone was watching them. Glancing over Matt's shoulder, she met the intense gaze of a man who was staring at them from the steps of the church. He had short blond hair and was wearing a green parka with a hood. Nancy had the feeling that she'd seen him before.

Then she remembered—he was an environmental activist. Giralda, that was his name. Tony Giralda. She had seen his face on posters for a campaign to clean up River Heights's Muskoka River.

Matt's voice drew Nancy's attention back to the conversation around her. "I'd like you all to come back to Glover's Corners," he was saying. "Rosemary has prepared enough food to feed an army." He gazed at the housekeeper affectionately, but she didn't return the look. She continued staring straight ahead, slightly dazed.

"Poor Mrs. Adams," Nancy said a few minutes later as she, Bess, and George climbed into Nancy's blue Mustang.

"What do you mean?" Bess asked. "She must be having one of the happiest days of her life. She was like a mother to Matt."

George stared at her cousin. "I didn't exactly see her falling all over him," she said dryly.

"That's because she's too stunned," Bess retorted.

They swung out onto the main street and followed the stream of cars heading toward the outskirts of River Heights. Glover's Corners lay between two heavily wooded areas and was bordered by a low brick wall. The entrance drive curved into the property from a tall, wrought-iron gate. The gate stood open, but the house itself was well hidden behind some gently rolling hills.

"This is just as I remember it," George said as Nancy turned onto the twisting drive.

After rounding a few curves, they could see the house. Built of rose-colored brick, it was huge, with a main hall and two wings stretching out on either side of it. The wings curved slightly toward the front, circling a large garden. The pond was barely visible at the foot of a gentle slope behind the house. The old stables and the pond, Nancy remembered, were behind the house.

Nancy parked behind the other cars and climbed out to crunch over the gravel path toward the front door. Other people were also making their way toward the house, and Nancy noticed that one of them was Tony Giralda. He was getting out of a battered-looking van a few cars in front of Nancy's Mustang.

"Pretty impressive," George said, once they were inside. The entrance hall was huge. Directly in front of them was a stately mahogany staircase. There were two curved archways leading to the two wings of the house to the right and left of the hall.

"The guests are all going this way," Bess said, pointing to the left.

"That's right," said Nancy. "As I remember, the other way leads to the more private areas."

There were several open doors along the hallway, and the girls peeked into them as they passed. There was a paneled library, a living room, and a smaller sitting room, all elegantly furnished. Most of the guests had collected in the formal dining room, so the girls went in there.

"Mrs. Adams sure seems to be a lot happier now," George commented.

The housekeeper was rushing around, seeing that the big urns were full of coffee and tea, fussing over the plates of cold meats and bowls of salad. Nancy saw that the color had come back to her face, and there was even a smile on her lips now.

"I don't know about you guys, but I'm starving," Nancy said, eyeing the long table that stretched along one wall. It was piled high with food.

The girls got in line and took plates. Nancy was just spooning some pasta salad onto hers when a deep voice spoke up right behind her: "I can't tell you how it feels to be back."

She turned to see Matt standing there. "It must be kind of weird for you," Nancy said. "How *does* it feel?"

Matt gave a deep sigh. "Wonderful and strange

at the same time. In some ways I feel as if I've never been away."

"Oh, but you have," Nancy said. "Five years is a long time." It was almost creepy to be talking to him again. If he really was Matt, she reminded herself.

He ran a hand through his thick black hair. "I guess so. I just wish I could have figured out who I was before . . ." He broke off.

Nancy gave him a sympathetic look. "Your father was a wonderful person," she said sincerely. "We'll all miss him." After a pause she asked, "How did you find out who you were?"

"I saw the obituary in the Chicago *Clarion,*" Matt explained. "There was a photo of my father, and as soon as I saw it I had to sit down. I knew he meant something to me, something very important. I read the obituary three times, and each time things came back more clearly. I don't think you can imagine what it felt like, Nancy."

"Very few people could," she admitted. "But then, very few people have amnesia."

"That's what your father said. I was talking to him before you got here. He said he's never run across a case in all the years he's practiced law."

This might not be amnesia, either, Nancy thought, if he's not the real Matt Glover. Almost instantly she felt aggravated with herself for raising the doubt so automatically. Lighten up, Drew, she scolded herself.

"I'm starving," Matt said, breaking into her thoughts. He filled his plate, then started to make himself a thick roast beef sandwich. As she watched him, Nancy suddenly remembered something.

Everyone had always teased Matt about the huge mounds of mustard he added to just about everything. She paid close attention, holding her breath as he clamped the top piece of bread over the beef.

Matt didn't bite into it, though. Heading for the silver bowls filled with brown and yellow mustard, he opened his sandwich and plastered the beef with mustard the way the real Matt Glover would have.

Nancy shook herself for being so untrusting. So far there wasn't really any reason to doubt him. Matt was speaking with Bess now in a completely casual and natural manner.

Seeing her father across the room, Nancy crossed to him, but as they talked her eyes kept straying to Matt and Bess. Bess seemed to be doing most of the talking, and from the smiles on both their faces, they were enjoying each other's company quite a bit.

"Is something bothering you, Nancy?" her father asked. "I just asked you a question, and you didn't even hear me."

Nancy felt herself blush. "Sorry, Dad. I was just thinking, it's pretty amazing about Matt coming back. Maybe it *is* him." She told him about the mustard.

Carson Drew followed her gaze. "A really clever impostor would know all about the person he's pretending to be," he replied, sounding thoughtful. "I honestly don't know what to think about him, Nancy. If you asked me whether that guy is Matt Glover or a con man, I couldn't give you an answer. Not yet."

Nancy took a bite of her pasta salad. "I guess the important thing is not to be biased either way."

"One thing's sure—he knows the house inside and out. When he first came here today, Rosemary said she asked him to get two trays for her from the second pantry. He got them in record time—not a false move."

Nancy thought of the huge kitchen with its many storage rooms and pantries in the back hall. It wouldn't be easy for a stranger to find the second pantry so quickly—unless he'd studied a blueprint of Glover's Corners.

"What's this about false moves?" George asked, coming up to Nancy and her father.

"We were just talking about Matt, and how he hasn't made any yet," Nancy told her.

"If he's an impostor, you mean," George added. "Well, so far he has two definite fans."

"You don't have to tell me who one of them

is," Nancy said with a laugh, nodding toward Bess. "Who's the other?"

"Mrs. Adams. I just heard her say something like, 'Maybe dreams *do* come true.' "

"She'd know better than anyone," Carson Drew commented. Putting his arm around Nancy's shoulders, he said, "I'm worn out. You girls won't mind if I leave early, will you?"

"Poor Dad," Nancy said. "Settling Mr. Glover's estate has been a lot of extra work for you, hasn't it? Here, I'll get your coat."

Out in the hall, Nancy paused to glance out the windows on either side of the front door. The day appeared to be colder and grayer than ever, and the cars lining the winding drive were covered with a frozen mist.

Shivering slightly, she went to the front hall closet and pulled her father's heavy overcoat from its hanger. She was just slinging it over one arm when a noise behind her made her pause.

Nancy swiveled around and saw someone emerge from the shadows near the front door. She recognized Tony Giralda's lean, wiry form as he strode toward her.

"So, you've been taken in by him, too," he said. Nancy saw that he had brown eyes, and there was a look of intense anger in them. In fact, it seemed to Nancy that his whole body was tense with a kind of nervous energy.

"What do you mean?" Nancy asked him.

"You're some kind of detective, right?" he

asked, but his angry voice made it sound like an accusation.

Nancy nodded.

Giralda's hands balled into fists at his sides. "I knew Matt Glover," he said, drawing the words out. "I knew him like my own brother. And that guy's not him."

Chapter

Three

"Hᴏᴡ ᴄᴀɴ ʏᴏᴜ ᴛᴇʟʟ?" Nancy asked Tony. "What kind of proof do you—"

"I've got to go," he said suddenly. "If you want to talk, you can find me at my office. Giralda's Environmental Action."

"Tomorrow?" Nancy asked immediately. If Tony Giralda had any proof that the man inside wasn't Matt Glover, she wanted to know what it was as soon as possible.

He nodded. "Hours are noon until eight. I'll be there all afternoon."

When Nancy went back into the library with her father's coat, Carson Drew was nowhere in sight. George was just putting her empty plate with some others at one end of the long table.

"Did you see where my dad went?" Nancy asked, going over to her.

George pointed toward a doorway at the rear of the dining room, which Nancy knew led to the kitchen. "He went back there with Mrs. Adams."

The two girls found Nancy's father in the kitchen, holding Mrs. Adams awkwardly in his arms and patting her back. The housekeeper's eyes were red rimmed, and she had obviously been crying.

When Mrs. Adams saw Nancy, she said, "Oh, dear, please excuse me. I feel like smiling and crying at the same time."

"Rosemary is feeling a bit overwhelmed," Nancy's father said.

Straightening herself, Mrs. Adams stepped away from Carson Drew and wiped her eyes with one end of the kitchen towel she was holding. "At first I couldn't be sure that young man was really Matt, and yet I wanted him to be. I wanted it so much."

She sat down at the long oak table. "Mr. Glover was a very fine man," she went on after a long pause. "He took it so hard when Matt disappeared. My heart ached for him. He was a wonderful employer, but things were never the same here after Matt vanished. You remember, Nancy, dear, how happy the atmosphere at the Corners was. The picnics and barbecues, the skating . . ."

"Yes," Nancy said in a comforting voice. "My friends and I were talking about it earlier. Mr.

Glover continued to invite us out here, but it was never the same after Matt died."

"We have to stop saying that now, of course," Mrs. Adams said, smiling. "Matt didn't die, thank goodness, and now he's come home. It's just wonderful, isn't it? If only his father could have lived to see him again." She looked as if she might start crying again, but then she clapped one hand over her mouth and said, "Silly me, it was only because of Mr. G's death that Matt remembered who he was."

"Yes, he told me how the article in the *Clarion* sparked his memory," Nancy said. She paused, then asked, "Tell me, Mrs. Adams. When did you know he really was Matt?"

"I began to suspect it when we came back here after the funeral. He stepped into the hall and asked me where the old elephant's leg was." Mrs. Adams was beaming, unaware of the puzzled expressions on the others' faces.

"Elephant's leg?" Carson Drew inquired.

"Yes, the old umbrella stand. Mr. G's father brought it back from Africa years ago. It was a hollowed-out leg—a curio, really. Matt always loved it as a child. I had to tell him his father gave it away after he disappeared. Mr. Glover couldn't stand being reminded of Matt every time he saw the thing."

"I wonder why he didn't ask yesterday, when he first came to the door?" Nancy said.

Mrs. Adams appeared to be indignant. "You

don't think I let him into the hall yesterday?" she asked. "He didn't take one step inside, because I couldn't be sure who he really was."

"But now you're sure?"

The housekeeper nodded. "When we came back here today, he knew right where to find my trays, for one thing. And when he went up to see his old room, he came back amazed at how it hadn't changed. Only a boy who'd been raised here could know such things, don't you agree?"

Nancy smiled rather than answering.

"Still," Mrs. Adams continued, "there's always that little nagging doubt, isn't there? A fortune hunter could learn about the umbrella stand and about how Matt's father kept the room the way it had been. . . . "

"And where the trays were kept in the second pantry," Nancy added.

Rosemary Adams wiped at some imaginary dirt on the table with the kitchen towel. "But I really knew in my heart that he was Matt when he called me Addie."

"Addie?" Nancy asked.

"That was Matt's private nickname for me. He didn't use it when other people were around, but in private, he always called me Addie."

Mrs. Adams glanced at her watch, then got quickly to her feet. "My goodness, I've been neglecting my guests," she said.

"Don't try to do too much," Carson Drew advised her.

"Oh, but there'll be lots of work now that Matthew is back," she sang out in a happy voice.

"So you think he'll stay on here?" George asked. "This place is pretty big for one person."

"Two people, you mean," Mrs. Adams corrected. "Don't forget, Matthew will surely want to marry and raise a family, and I'd want to stay on and take care of them."

Nancy gazed after Mrs. Adams as she bustled back toward the dining room. The detective in her was beginning to be very intrigued by this situation. Whether or not the man she'd met that day really was Matt Glover, his appearance was definitely causing ripples.

"Did you ever hear Matt call Mrs. Adams 'Addie'?" George asked from the backseat of Nancy's car. She and Nancy and Bess were driving back toward town from Glover's Corners.

"I don't think so," Nancy said, "but Mrs. Adams said that he didn't use the name in front of other people."

"What's this Addie business?" Bess asked.

"Matt's private nickname for Mrs. Adams," George told her. She stretched her long legs out on the seat and leaned back. "It seemed funny to me, that's all."

"*I* think it sounds cute," Bess countered.

George rolled her eyes. "You think everything about Matt is cute."

"That's because it is," Bess replied. "Matt's a major heartthrob, you have to admit."

"He is handsome," Nancy agreed. She gave Bess a sideways glance. "But maybe you should hold off falling in love with the guy until everyone's sure he really is Matt."

"Who's not sure?" Bess asked. "Mrs. Adams is convinced. Who would know him better? And you saw how much mustard he put on his sandwich. How would he know how much Matt liked mustard unless he *is* Matt?"

"Well, Tony Giralda's not so sure." Nancy told Bess and George about the environmentalist's reservations.

Bess looked at her doubtfully. "Well, I don't remember anyone named Tony Giralda hanging around with Matt. How would he know?"

"Tony said he knew Matt like a brother," Nancy explained. "We were a lot younger than they were, don't forget. We don't know who Matt's friends were."

"Yeah," said George. "Just because we didn't know him doesn't mean Matt didn't."

Nancy steered the Mustang onto Bess's street and pulled up in front of her house. "Anyway, I'm going to talk to him tomorrow and find out what he has to say. It can't hurt."

"I don't see why you guys can't just admit that Matt's really back." Bess got out of the car, pausing with the door open while she looked back and forth from Nancy to George. "I would think you'd at least believe Mrs. Adams if you don't believe me. Oh, well. See you." She closed the door and was gone.

Nancy dropped George off and was on the way home when a new thought struck her. It was something Mrs. Adams had said: "Don't forget, Matthew will surely want to marry and raise a family, and I'd want to stay on and take care of them."

Mrs. Adams had lived at Glover's Corners for over twenty years, and she loved the place. Where would she go if the estate was given to River Heights as a museum or a nursing home or if it was demolished to make room for development?

It was definitely in the housekeeper's best interests to have Matt show up. She knew Matt better than any other living person and could easily teach a stranger—a stranger who looked just like Matt—all the little things. Maybe she'd even made up that stuff about her nickname being Addie.

Nancy didn't want to believe it, but a part of her was whispering that the only one who knew enough about Matt and Glover's Corners to set up a giant fraud was Mrs. Adams.

Chapter

Four

Nᴀɴᴄʏ ʟᴇᴛ ᴏᴜᴛ a long breath. She could hardly believe that Mrs. Adams would deceive anyone, but she had to admit that it was possible.

A dog ran out into the road. Nancy swerved to avoid it, then forced herself to keep her mind focused on her driving for the rest of the way home.

She found a note from her father in the kitchen: "Went to bed early. See you in the ᴀ.ᴍ." Beneath it, he had scrawled, "Call Bess."

Picking up the kitchen extension, she dialed Bess's number, smiling to herself when her friend's bubbly voice came over the line.

"Nan! I have so much to tell you!"

Nancy leaned against the kitchen counter and cradled the receiver between her head and shoulder. "I just dropped you off ten minutes ago, Bess. How much could there be to say?"

"Matt called," Bess said, her voice shrill with excitement. "He told me how much it meant to him to have good friends like me after being away for five years. He mentioned you and George, too."

Nancy could practically see her friend's grin over the line. "I forgot to tell you guys on the ride home," Bess went on, "that he had told me his whole story—well, practically all."

"What did he tell you?"

Nancy listened to the story about the obituary to see if he'd told it any differently to Bess, but it was the same, almost word for word. "He doesn't remember the skiing accident in Colorado at all," Bess finished. "He didn't even know his own name until he read it in the paper. He had taken the name Gary Page. He was working as a journalist. Doesn't that sound familiar?"

"Yeah," Nancy agreed. "I remember that Matt was the editor of the high school paper. I think he even wrote a few articles for the *Morning Record.*"

"So that's more proof he's really Matt, right?"

"Maybe," Nancy said noncommittally. "Where'd he work? In Colorado?"

"He didn't say. He just said something made him want to keep moving east. He worked on a paper in Nebraska for two years, and then he went to Iowa before going to work for the *Clarion* in Chicago."

They talked for a few more minutes, and then Nancy hung up. It seemed more and more as if Matt was who he said he was. It would be great if he were—especially for Bess—but Nancy knew she wouldn't be convinced until she had checked out a few things. Tony Giralda's doubts, for one.

Maybe she'd go to the Chicago *Clarion* office, too, to check on his background to see if Gary Page was the same guy as the Matt Glover she'd met that day.

Her father would be checking him out, too. Carson Drew was spending the whole next day with Matt. Apparently there were matters to be settled before Matt could be legally accepted as Clayton Glover's heir. If anyone could catch him in a lie, it was Carson Drew.

Nancy shook her head. She'd thought about Matt Glover enough for one day. She knew one way to get her mind off him. Grabbing the bag with her disassembled tape deck in it, Nancy sat down at the kitchen table, dumped the parts out, and concentrated on putting them back together.

When Nancy woke in the morning, light snow-flakes were dancing outside her window. She had stayed up until after two A.M., working on her tape deck, and had slept much later than usual. It was ten by the time she had dressed in jeans and a pale green cable-knit sweater and went down-stairs.

Hannah Gruen, the Drews' housekeeper, was making chicken soup for lunch. Hannah had been living with the Drews since Nancy's mother died, when Nancy was just three, and she was more like a member of the family than a house-keeper.

"That smells delicious," Nancy said, sniffing appreciatively.

"Your father's at his office with that young man who says he's Clayton Glover's son," Hannah informed her. "I imagine they'll be there all day."

Pouring herself a glass of orange juice, Nancy popped two slices of bread into the toaster. "What do you think?" she asked.

"About what?"

"About the new Matt," Nancy said. "Do you think it's possible to have amnesia for five years and snap out of it when you see your father's obituary?"

Hannah considered Nancy's question. "It hap-pens all the time on TV," she said, "which is enough for me to doubt it. On the other hand, *anything* is possible."

"I guess you're right—on both counts," Nancy said, laughing. When her toast popped up, she buttered it, then smothered it with strawberry jam.

"You're going to spoil your appetite for lunch," Hannah told her.

Nancy took a bite of toast. "Don't worry. I always have room for your soup."

At twelve Nancy proved it, eating a big bowl full of it. After mopping up the last of the soup with a thick slice of crusty bread, she checked her watch. It was early afternoon, and Tony Giralda would probably be in his office by now.

Pulling on her leather boots and heavy jacket, Nancy grabbed her tape deck from the small table in the front hall, where she'd left it the night before. Then she ran out to her car. A light snow was falling, but the flakes melted as soon as they hit the ground. Backing out of the driveway, Nancy put a tape in the deck and was pleased to hear that the sound was perfect and that the machine was no longer eating tapes.

Nancy drove toward the address she'd looked up for Giralda's Environmental Action office. Soon she pulled up in front of a building on the outskirts of River Heights's downtown area.

To call the Environmental Action building an office was stretching things a bit, Nancy thought as she studied the building through the window of her car. It was really just a long, low garage. Posters publicizing Tony's campaign to clean up the Muskoka River covered the area around the door.

Pulling the fleecy collar of her leather jacket

close around her ears, Nancy stepped out of the car, walked to the door, and knocked on it. A few seconds later Tony opened it.

"I was wondering if you'd show up," he said as she stepped inside.

It wasn't exactly an enthusiastic hello, Nancy thought, but at least his voice had lost some of the angry intensity of the day before.

"I said I would," she told him.

He took her jacket and hung it on a hook just inside the door next to his parka. Then Nancy followed him down a small hallway lined with closed doors. Nancy guessed they opened into closets—there really wasn't room for much more.

Tony led Nancy into an office. The room was crammed with posters and buttons. A table against the wall was piled high with letters and envelopes and so was the only desk in the room.

"This is pretty much a one-man operation," Tony explained. "I can't afford to hire anyone full time, so I have to depend on volunteers." He gestured around the empty office. "As you can see, they're not always dependable." Clearing off some posters that were on his desk chair, he offered Nancy the seat, while he leaned on the edge of the desk.

Nancy got right to the point. "You said you were convinced that the man at Glover's Corners isn't the real Matthew Glover."

"That's right—he's not," Tony replied.

"Do you have any evidence?"

Tony crossed his arms over his chest, and that dark, brooding look came back into his eyes. "Well, not hard evidence," he told her. "But I *know* that guy is a phony."

More opinion, Nancy thought. Opinion was a long way from being concrete proof. "Do you mean he doesn't look like Matt or sound like him?" she prodded.

"Oh, he looks like Matt would look now, if Matt were alive, and he sounds the way I remember Matt's voice. But he's not Matt."

"In other words, it's just a feeling you have?" Nancy said, trying to keep her disappointment out of her voice. This was turning out to be a total waste of time.

Tony nodded. "It's not just a feeling. It's a *gut* feeling, as strong as they come."

"Too bad they don't allow gut feelings to be admitted as evidence in court," she said. The words sounded more sarcastic than she had meant them to be, and Tony shot her an angry look.

"I'm sorry," Nancy said quickly, "but if you could just think of what it is that makes you so sure he's a fake, that would help. Was it the way he walked or some gesture he made? Matt was left-handed, according to my dad. I watched that guy yesterday, and he favored his left hand, too. But maybe there are some things like that that don't fit. Can you think of anything?"

Tony raked his fingers nervously through his short blond hair. "I can't think of anything specific, but I swear to you I'm right."

Great, Nancy thought. Getting up from the chair, she told him, "I don't see what you think I can do to help."

He pounded his hand on the desk so hard that Nancy jumped. "Can't you get to the truth about this guy?" he blurted out. Recovering himself, he went on more calmly. "I mean, you must have ways of working so that he wouldn't suspect you."

Nancy shook her head. "If he's an impostor, he'll suspect everyone. I'm sorry, but unless you can give me something more concrete to go on, there's nothing I can do." She stood up to leave.

Tony made a disgusted noise in his throat and turned away. Nancy walked out, casting a glance back over her shoulder. Tony's face was set in an angry grimace.

Nancy was surprised to find her father home when she returned from Tony Giralda's office. He was sitting at the kitchen table, eating a bowl of Hannah's soup. Nancy sat with him.

"I thought you were going to be tied up with Matt Glover all day," she said. "It's only one-thirty."

"I had to come back to pick up some papers," Carson said, tipping his bowl to scoop up the last of the soup. "You know, Matt is coming through with flying colors so far," he told her. "He signed an affidavit, and the signature compares well with Matt's. There's a slight difference, but handwriting changes over time. Of course, I'll submit a sample of the writing to an expert, just to be sure."

"Did he sign with his left hand?" Nancy asked.

"Yes, and he did it completely naturally." Carson pushed the empty bowl away from him and then sighed. "Going over the writing samples could take a few days. It's a touchy situation, so we have to be very careful. Clayton's will is clear that his son is to inherit everything if he's ever found. That's usual in cases where a body hasn't been recovered. If Matt hadn't shown up, Glover's money was to be split up among several charities."

"He didn't leave any to Mrs. Adams?" Nancy asked.

"Oh, there's a nice bequest to Rosemary," he said. "But the rest, which amounts to several million dollars, was to go to charity."

"I suppose he left money to the hospital," Nancy guessed.

"Yes. There's also a large bequest to the hospital's day-care center and several bequests to smaller organizations and businesses."

A sudden idea occurred to Nancy. Leaning forward over the kitchen table, she asked, "I don't suppose Tony Giralda's Environmental Action group would be one of them?"

Carson was surprised. "Yes," he said. "As a matter of fact, it is. How did you know?"

Nancy told her father about her visit to the Environmental Action office. "From the look of the place, I can bet he has a hard time making ends meet. But he's incredibly devoted to his work. He seems practically fanatical about it."

"A hefty bequest from Mr. Glover could be the answer to his financial problems," Carson put in. "I see what you're getting at, Nancy."

Nancy's blue eyes were wide. "Maybe Tony Giralda is fierce enough about his work to want to cheat the real Matt out of his legitimate inheritance!"

Chapter

Five

I T'S A POSSIBILITY, NANCY," Carson told her.
"There's just one—"

Nancy didn't hear because she had already
jumped up from the table and was heading for
the front door. "I can hardly wait to tell Bess and
George," she said excitedly as she grabbed her
jacket from the closet. "See you later, Dad."

She drove over and picked up Bess, and then
they went directly to George's.

"You mean Tony Giralda might be trying to
frame Matt so he can get Mr. Glover's money?"
Bess said after Nancy had told them about her
encounter with Tony and the bequest to his
organization. "That's disgusting!"

"Tony Giralda's not the only one who might be
cheating to get a piece of the Glover fortune,

either," Nancy went on. She explained her idea about Mrs. Adams coaching someone to play the role of Matt.

George brushed a hand through her short, dark curls and seemed extremely dubious. "I don't know, Nan. She seemed harmless to me."

"Maybe," Nancy said. "The point is, whatever we're dealing with, there may be more people involved in it than just Matt. I'm going to keep an eye on Tony Giralda and Mrs. Adams—and I think I need to check out Matt, too."

"Where do we start?" George asked.

"Well, I'd like to check out Gary Page's credentials at the Chicago *Clarion*," Nancy suggested.

George looked at her watch. "If we leave right now, we could be back by early evening."

"Well, *I* already believe Matt," Bess said. "But if it'll make you guys feel better, let's go."

Nancy frowned. "I wish we had a photo of him to take with us, to show the people at the paper."

"No problem," said Bess, blushing a little. "I just happen to have a very recent picture of him." She fumbled in her purse and drew out an instant photo of Matt.

"Where did you get that?" Nancy and George asked at the same time.

"I went over to the Corners this morning," Bess said, her whole face bright pink now. "When Matt called last night, he said I should feel free to stop by, so I did. Mrs. Adams was snapping pictures of Matt and gave me one."

"Pretty good detecting, Bess," Nancy joked. "It's just what we need. Let's go."

Bess grinned. "And I thought I was just flirting!"

The light snow had let up, so the three friends made good time. The *Clarion* offices were in the Loop, or downtown Chicago, and were in a building about five times as big as the one where the River Heights *Morning Record* was.

At the main receptionist's desk they were directed to the sixth floor, where another receptionist asked them what they wanted.

"We'd like to speak to someone about a reporter who worked here until a few days ago," Nancy said. "Gary Page."

The receptionist spoke into a phone, then told them, "Ms. McCoy will be with you in a moment."

They could hear heels tapping smartly down a hall, and then a tall woman with shoulder-length black hair came into the reception area. "I'm Sheila McCoy," she said. "I was Gary's editor—" She caught herself, then added, "I guess I should start calling him Matt Glover. I hope nothing's happened to him?"

Nancy introduced herself and assured Sheila McCoy that he was fine. "How long had he worked for you?" Nancy asked as the editor led her, Bess, and George back to her desk in the newsroom.

"About a year. He came with excellent references from a paper in Iowa City. He was a good reporter, and I'll miss him. They don't grow on trees, you know."

She opened a file and took out a cutting. "I don't think I've ever seen any reporter with a better memory for detail. Here, this is a copy of one of the first stories he did for the *Clarion*. It's about a local entrepreneur—kind of a rags-to-riches story."

Nancy glanced at the article with the Gary Page byline but didn't notice anything special about it. "What about his past?" she asked, looking up from the article. "Did Gary Page ever talk about his family or background?"

Sheila shook her head. "No," she said. "He was *very* private. To say that he kept to himself would be an understatement."

Pulling Bess's photo from her purse, Nancy asked Sheila if it was a good likeness of Gary Page. This time Sheila's eyes narrowed. "What's this all about, anyway?" she asked.

"We're, uh, working on an article for our local paper," Nancy lied. "Matt Glover's a real human-interest story back in River Heights—that's where we're from."

The smile returned to Sheila's face. "Well, good luck," she told them. "Great shot," she added after studying the picture. "Looks just like him."

"May I keep this?" Nancy asked, holding up the article.

"Sure." Sheila shook hands with them. "Say hello to Gary—I mean, Matt, for me."

"Now we have all the proof we need," Bess said, stirring her hot cocoa. After they'd left the *Clarion,* they had decided to stop at a diner for something to eat and drink before making the drive back to River Heights.

"Hold on," Nancy said. "We need to find out a lot more." She took a sip of her cocoa and stared out the window next to their booth. "All Sheila McCoy told us was that the man in the snapshot was the man she knew as Gary Page. That doesn't mean the guy is really Matt Glover."

"Well, at least he told the truth when he said he'd worked at the *Clarion,*" George said. She was flipping through the jukebox selections at their table.

Nancy pulled out the article the newspaper editor had given her and skimmed through it. It was dated a little over a year earlier and was about some man who had once been a gardener for a private estate. He had opened up a landscape gardening business in downtown Chicago and had become very successful.

"It's very well written," said Bess, reading over her shoulder.

There was a picture of the man, Jake Loomis,

but since it was a photocopy, the picture was a blur. Nothing about the article was helpful, and Nancy folded it and put it back in her jacket pocket.

"You know," George said, "that woman said something funny—about Gary Page being a loner."

Nancy nodded. "I was wondering about that, too. I mean, what kind of guy *never* mentions anything about his background during a whole year? Sheila McCoy saw him practically every day, but she says she knows nothing about him."

"Somebody might act like that if he planned to vanish," George proposed, downing the last of her cocoa. "A man who planned to impersonate someone who was dead wouldn't want people to know anything about him."

"Oh, come on, you guys," Bess cut in. "He had amnesia, remember. How could he tell anyone about his life? *He* didn't know anything about it."

Bess glanced out the diner window, and suddenly delighted surprise lit up her face. "Look!" she exclaimed. "There he is—in that phone booth!"

Following Bess's gaze, Nancy immediately saw Matt's unmistakable figure. He was speaking into a pay phone a few yards from the diner. There was a vintage sports roadster beside him, and Nancy recognized it as having belonged to Mr. Glover.

"What's he doing here?" George wanted to know.

"We'll know soon enough," Bess said, waving out the window until she got his attention. "He's coming over."

Matt was wearing a broad grin as he hung up the phone and headed for the diner. "Hi, you guys," he said cheerfully. He spoke to all of them, but Nancy noticed that he saved the fullest force of his deep blue eyes for Bess, and she was eating up the attention.

"What a treat," he told her. "I get to see you twice in one day." He leaned close to her and said jokingly, "We've got to stop meeting like this."

"Not if I can help it," Bess returned, laughing.

Nancy glanced across the table at George, who rolled her eyes as if to say, "She's really getting silly about this guy!"

Nancy knew just what George meant, but she wasn't sure what to do about it. "Um, I'll be right back, you guys. I'm just going to the ladies' room," she said.

She gave George a meaningful look as she got up and was glad when George said, "I'll come with you."

"Can you believe it?" George said, leaning against the sink when she and Nancy were alone in the ladies' room. "Bess adores that guy. She's only just met him again—I mean, if he really is Matt—and she practically worships him."

"I noticed Matt doesn't seem to mind a bit,"

Nancy added. "In fact, he seems to be egging her on. This could turn out to be a real disaster."

George nodded. "I know what you mean. What if he is a phony and just using Bess to gain credibility?" Her brown eyes were filled with concern. "I'd hate to see her get hurt."

Nancy nodded. "That's what I'm afraid of, too. For her sake, I hope Matt Glover really is who he says he is. Because if we prove that he's not, it will break Bess's heart."

Chapter

Six

WHAT DO YOU THINK we should do?" George asked.

"I think we'd better hurry up and find out the truth about Matt. Come on," Nancy said, reaching for the ladies' room door. "Let's get back to the table before Bess decides to elope with the guy!"

George laughed, but her expression became grim again when she and Nancy returned to their seats and saw the adoration written across Bess's face.

"Uh-oh," Nancy whispered. "We'd better break this up."

She cleared her throat loudly as she and George sat down again. Matt and Bess broke off their conversation to acknowledge them.

"I have to tell you," Nancy said to Matt, "that the reason we're in Chicago is because of you."

"Nancy!" Bess gasped, shocked. She looked nervously at Matt, obviously not wanting him to know they'd been snooping on him. Matt was staring in bewilderment at Nancy.

"It's important for us to be honest with you, Matt," Nancy explained. "We were checking up on you at the *Clarion.*"

"I told Nancy it wasn't necessary," Bess put in quickly.

Matt smiled at all of them. "Actually, I'm glad you checked up on me. I want you to trust me, and you're right, Nancy, we have to be honest with one another."

"Good," said Nancy. "I'm glad we understand each other."

"As a matter of fact, I asked your father if I could take a lie-detector test," Matt added to Nancy.

"Then everyone will have to believe you," said Bess.

He grinned at her again, then said, "Let's talk about something more pleasant."

"Like what?" Bess's eyes were shining.

"Like ice skating. The temperature out there must have dropped ten degrees since noon. The pond at home should be nicely frozen over tonight. What would you all say to a moonlight ice-skating party?"

"Just like the old days," Bess said.

"It's a great idea," Nancy said. The more they hung out with Matt, the more certain they could be that he was—or wasn't—Mr. Glover's son.

"Good." Matt got up to go. "I have to get back to the Corners and sweep the pond for tonight. The car holds only two, I'm afraid. Would you like to ride back to River Heights with me, Bess?"

Nancy held her breath, hoping that her friend would refuse.

"Sure," Bess replied breathlessly. "I'd love to."

"I'll pick you up in an hour, after I check in at home," Nancy told George as she dropped her off at her house.

After a quick hello to her father and Hannah, Nancy decided to go see Tony Giralda again. She had almost an hour before she had to pick up George and Bess, and she wanted to check out her theory that Tony might be trying to cheat Matt out of his inheritance.

Nancy changed her cable-knit sweater for a turtleneck and heavy ski sweater. She grabbed her skates and was almost out the door when the phone rang. She answered it in the kitchen.

"Ned!" she said, a smile lighting up her face when she heard her boyfriend's voice on the other end of the line. "Where are you?"

"Still at school. That's why I'm calling. I'm

afraid I won't be able to make it out to see you this weekend. I've got a killer test on Monday, and I've got to stay here and study. Sorry."

"That's okay," she said. "But I hope you know you'll have to make it up to me by being doubly sweet the next time you come, Nickerson."

It felt great to talk to him, and soon Nancy found herself telling Ned about Matt Glover.

"Yeah, I read about him showing up in the paper," Ned said when she was done. His voice was filled with concern as he added, "If he's an impostor, he's got a lot to lose if anyone exposes him. Be careful, Nan."

"You know me," she said in a teasing voice.

He sighed. "That's what has me worried."

Nancy said goodbye, then hung up and went out to her Mustang. It was already dark, but the porch light illuminated the outdoor thermometer, which read fifteen degrees. The pond would definitely be frozen.

Raising her eyes, she admired the pale three-quarter moon that was just rising. She thought of the old days Matt kept mentioning. If only she knew whether he remembered them himself, or whether he'd been coached to memorize the details of Matt Glover's boyhood by someone else. She remembered Sheila McCoy saying that Gary Page had the best memory for detail she'd ever known. Was it good enough to memorize all the details of someone else's life?

As Nancy pulled up in front of the Environmental Action office, it was just before eight and she stopped thinking about Matt and started thinking about Tony. She frowned when she looked at the office. She didn't see any lights on. Maybe he'd left right on time that day.

Looking up and down the street, she saw that it was deserted and pitch-dark except for the weak glow of a street lamp a block away. Nancy reached into the glove compartment for her flashlight and flicked it on, before walking through the frigid night air to the office door.

She knocked and called Tony's name, but no one answered. Next, she tried the door. It opened. Great! She'd just take a quick look around for anything incriminating. Shining her flashlight so she could see where she was going, Nancy went down the short hallway, past the two closed doors, toward the garagelike office.

The door to Tony's office stood wide open, but the lights were off. In a soft voice, Nancy tentatively called his name again, just to make sure no one was there. Then she swung her beam around the room.

After flipping through the papers on his desk, she opened the top drawer. Nothing there but a candy bar and some old papers that had to do with a local law about industrial dumping into the river.

The other drawers were just as uninteresting, and they were dirty, too. Her nose began to feel itchy from all the dust she was creating.

Just then Nancy felt a prickly sensation at the back of her neck. It didn't make sense that Giralda had left the building unlocked, so he must be coming back soon. She knew she should leave, but she wanted to check out whatever was beyond the other doors leading off the hallway. Doing so was probably a waste of time, but she couldn't pass up the opportunity.

Quickly she went back to the hallway, swinging the beam of her flashlight back and forth. When she reached the first door, she tried the handle gingerly. The door pulled open with a creak, and Nancy peered into the dim interior. It was a closet, as she'd expected. It contained nothing but cleaning supplies and an ancient-looking mimeograph machine.

At the next door Nancy paused for a moment. Was that a noise she heard? She stood completely still, listening, but there was nothing.

I guess I just imagined it, she thought, shaking her head. This place is starting to get me spooked. Resolutely, she pulled open the door and stepped inside.

All of a sudden Nancy felt herself being roughly shoved forward. She fell to her knees. A second later she heard the door slam shut behind her and the lock turn. She was trapped!

Nancy swung the beam of her flashlight until she found the light switch, then turned it on. Keeping the lights off didn't matter anymore, since someone knew she was there.

She didn't have time to wonder who, though, because just then she heard a low growling behind her. Nancy whirled around.

Standing in the back left corner of the room were two very large dogs. They looked part German shepherd and part something else—something wild. Their teeth were bared, and their fierce eyes were trained on Nancy!

Chapter

Seven

NANCY FROZE, trying to remember everything she knew about calming animals. "Good boys." She tried to keep her voice calm, but she could hear that it was higher pitched than normal. "What good boys, yes. There's nothing to be afraid of."

The dogs' teeth were no longer bared, she saw with relief, but they were still growling, so she kept talking. "I don't blame you for being angry at me. If someone burst into my house as I did into yours, I'd be furious. . . ." She trailed off, peering cautiously at the huge animals. Was it working?

She wasn't sure. "Good boys," she said again. The dogs seemed to be calming down, but Nancy wasn't—especially when she heard a voice outside the door shout, "Who's there?"

It was Tony Giralda! There was no way she could hide from him now, so she called out, "It's me—Nancy Drew."

There was a pause, then the door was unlocked and opened. Tony was standing in the hall, a frown on his face. "What are you doing in there?" he asked. "What are you doing here at all?"

"Get me away from these dogs, first," Nancy said, stepping quickly around him and into the hall. "I didn't know you had attack dogs."

"Attack dogs?" Tony repeated, looking amused. "Fred and Max wouldn't hurt a flea. They're high-strung, but they're sweethearts." As if to prove it, Tony whistled softly, and the big dogs loped over to him, giving little yowls of happiness when Tony petted them. "Fred was probably terrified when you went in there. He's afraid of strangers."

"I didn't go in, I was pushed," Nancy told Tony. "Hard." She gazed intently at him.

Tony's mouth dropped open. "But nobody was even here. I was out getting dinner. When I came back and saw the door was open, at first I was afraid a burglar was in here. But I guess I just left it unlocked." He smiled sheepishly. "Sometimes I get so caught up in my work I forget to lock up."

He led her back to his office, switching lights on as he went and checking out the entire area.

"Whoever pushed you is gone now," he said as they sat down, Nancy at his desk chair and Tony in a gray metal folding chair. "Did you get a look at the person?"

"No. Anyone could have gotten in the front door."

"Mmmm." Tony frowned. "Well, nothing seems to be missing, so I guess if the person was a burglar, you scared him off. Hey, you still haven't answered my question," he said. "What were *you* doing here?"

Nancy watched him for a second before answering. She wasn't sure, but it didn't seem as if Tony had been the one to push her. He seemed genuinely surprised to see her. Besides, why would he push her into Fred and Max's room if he knew the big dogs wouldn't harm her?

On the other hand, if he knew Nancy didn't know the dogs were harmless, he could have locked her in the room just to scare her or to teach her a lesson.

Nancy frowned. The only thing the incident did was reinforce her feeling that she was right to be looking into the Matt Glover case. Someone didn't like her snooping around, and someone had tried to do something about it.

"I wanted to see you," she told Tony at last. It was true, even if she did get in a little snooping while she was at it. "I wanted to ask you some questions."

"Like what?"

She decided to confide in Tony—up to a point. "I went to the offices of the *Clarion* in Chicago this afternoon," she said. "I spoke to Matt Glover's editor. She identified a photograph of him and confirmed everything he'd said."

Nancy took out the article Sheila McCoy had given her and handed it to Tony. "Here's a sample of one of his earliest pieces for the *Clarion*. He was using the name Gary Page then."

Tony smoothed the crumpled photocopy and scanned it briefly. He was about to hand it back when something caught his eye. "Jake Loomis!" he exclaimed. "I always wondered what happened to him. He left town a few years ago."

Nancy felt a prickling sensation along the top of her scalp. "Jake Loomis used to live in River Heights?" she asked.

"Sure. He was the gardener out at Glover's Corners. He worked there for years. Wow, this brings it all back! Yeah, Loomis must have left when Matt was about fifteen or sixteen. He always had dreams about setting up his own business."

"He seems to have succeeded, judging by this article."

"Yeah." Tony leaned forward and said in an urgent voice, "Look, this is all beside the point.

What I want to know is, what are you doing about exposing this fake Matt Glover? I mean, surely you can see by now that I'm right about him."

No, Nancy couldn't. She didn't know whom to believe. She didn't really trust Tony *or* Matt. Tony wanted Matt to be a fake, so that Giralda's Environmental Action would get a piece of Mr. Glover's fortune. Since he hadn't mentioned the money he'd be receiving from the estate, maybe he wasn't playing straight with her.

She wanted to find out more about Tony's interest in the will, but she was afraid of pressing her luck. She'd already been accosted once, and she didn't want to risk it happening again in such a deserted place. She rose to go. "Thanks for the information. I'll be in touch."

Tony walked her out to her car. The moon had fully risen, and the gloomy street in front of the office was now bathed in silvery light. Suddenly Nancy had an inspiration. Why not ask Tony to Matt's skating party? Maybe she could learn something from how Tony and Matt behaved toward each other.

Tony reacted oddly to her suggestion. He seemed shy and unsure of himself. "I don't know," he said. "I haven't really been invited. I'm not sure I should come."

"I'm inviting you," Nancy said. "If you don't have skates, there are probably some there you can borrow. Besides, I thought you said you knew Matt like a brother."

"The *real* Matt," Tony muttered. "Not this guy."

"That's the whole point. You'll be able to watch him on what's supposed to be his home turf. You can't afford to pass up a chance like this."

Tony rubbed his chin, considering. "Yeah, I guess you're right. Okay, I'll go," he said, but he didn't sound as though he really wanted to.

Nancy climbed into her car. "I have to pick up my friends first. Why don't you go ahead to the Corners and we'll meet you there."

Tony still seemed troubled, but he agreed.

Nancy couldn't help wondering why he was acting so strange. Why would he be reluctant to visit Matt—unless he had something to hide?

George was ready and waiting, dressed in red sweats and a heavy down vest. Her ice skates were slung over her shoulder, and she was eager to get on the ice. A natural athlete with terrific coordination, George was at her best when she was in action.

Five minutes later they were in front of Bess's house, and Bess, wearing a short pleated skirt, a pink turtleneck and tights, and a heavy sweater, was climbing into the backseat.

"Aren't you afraid you'll freeze in that?" George asked, gesturing at Bess's skirt.

"I have on three pairs of tights," Bess returned. She added in an anxious voice. "Do they make my legs look too fat?"

"Are you kidding? You look great!" Nancy said firmly. She was a little dismayed, though, because she knew exactly whom Bess wanted to look great *for*.

As they drove to Glover's Corners, Nancy told her friends about what had happened at Giralda's office. "Anyway, I invited him to come skating with us tonight," she said, finishing her story.

"What!" Bess and George exclaimed together.

"What did you do that for?" Bess went on.

"He has an interest in exposing Matt," Nancy said. "It may be greed on his part, or it may be something more honest. I have to find out."

"Oh, Nan," said Bess from the backseat. "Can't we forget about the case for tonight? I just want to have fun."

Nancy smiled at her in the rearview mirror. "Me, too. I'm just going to keep my eyes open, that's all." Turning into the driveway, she announced, "Here we are."

"Oh, it looks more gorgeous than usual," Bess said as they climbed out of the Mustang.

Nancy had to agree. Glover's Corners was blazing with light from every window. There were white Christmas-tree lights strung in the bare limbs of the trees around the pond, and the moon had climbed high, shedding a warm glow on the skeletal maple trees and the carefully trimmed evergreen bushes by the house.

Suddenly Nancy blinked. "That's it," she said softly.

"What's it?" asked George.

Nancy quickly explained what Tony Giralda had told her about Jake Loomis's being the gardener at Glover's Corners. "You know, I thought there was something funny, and I just realized what it is."

Nancy took a deep breath, then went on. "All the article said was that Loomis had worked at a private estate. Mr. Glover's name was never even mentioned, even though, according to Tony, Jake Loomis worked there for many years. Don't you think that's weird?"

"Why?" Bess looked confused.

"Loomis is a pretty successful guy now," George said. "Maybe he didn't mention Glover's Corners because he wanted to play down the fact that he used to be a gardener for a rich guy. It might be embarrassing for him."

"Maybe," Nancy said slowly. "But what if Gary Page or Matt Glover—whoever he is—*purposely* didn't mention Glover's Corners in the article. What if he didn't want anything to connect Jake Loomis to the Glover family?"

"What are you getting at, Nan?" Bess was stamping her feet to keep warm.

Nancy took a deep breath. "It's quite possible that a fake Matt Glover and Jake Loomis are working *together* to steal Mr. Glover's fortune!"

Chapter

Eight

INDIGNATION PLAYED OVER Bess's face.

"That's ridicu—" she started to say, but she broke off in midword, startled by a hissing noise from the darkness behind them.

"Pssst!"

Nancy, Bess, and George whirled around to see Tony Giralda step into the light of one of the lanterns lining the front drive. Nancy hadn't noticed his van when they drove up, but now she saw that it was parked under one of the huge, leafless maple trees.

"Why didn't you go in?" Nancy asked him.

"I don't know those people. I was waiting for you."

"But you must know Mrs. Adams—if you and Matt were such good friends," she said, studying

61

him curiously. "I thought you said you knew him like a brother."

The way that Tony scuffed his feet in the gravel told Nancy that he'd been lying. But why? "Well, forget it," she said after a minute. "Let's just go in. It's freezing out here."

Matt was waiting for them in the library. He looked amazingly handsome in dark pants and a royal blue ski sweater. The fire was roaring, and there was an enormous plate of sandwiches on the low table. The air smelled of cloves and cinnamon, and Nancy realized that Mrs. Adams must have revived one of her favorite recipes, mulled cider.

Matt gave them all a big hello. Then, turning to Tony, he said, "I'm glad you came, Tony. It's been a long time since we skated together."

Tony hesitated before he took Matt's hand, and when he shook it, it was with a strictly formal air. Then he went and sat stiffly in a leather chair.

Mrs. Adams came in a moment later, holding a freshly baked pie. "Hello, girls," she said. "This is a special night, with the house full of young people again."

She put the pie down on a silver stand and straightened. Her gaze landed on Tony, and she peered at him with a puzzled expression on her face.

"This is Tony Giralda, Addie," Matt said smoothly. "You must remember him."

"Yes," she said vaguely. "You were here after Mr. Glover's funeral, weren't you?"

Tony rose from his seat and nodded, an embarrassed flush in his cheeks.

So Tony *had* been lying, Nancy thought. Surely Mrs. Adams would have recognized him from the old days if he had known Matt as well as he'd said he had.

Matt broke the uneasy silence after Mrs. Adams left the room. "I thought we should get in some carbo-loading before we skate," he said, cutting into the pie and handing out plates to everyone.

"Definitely," Bess agreed. She took a big bite of her pie. Giggling, she added, "We wouldn't want to collapse from lack of energy."

As Nancy dug into her own slice, she couldn't help but admire Matt's friendly, easy way. He urged them to help themselves to sandwiches and went to the kitchen to bring back a tray with mugs for the mulled cider. It was easy to see why Bess was attracted to him.

"Don't get too comfortable," Matt warned them after a few minutes. He picked up a blue woolen hat and a pair of gloves and pulled them on. "We have some serious skating to do."

"All right!" said George, jumping to her feet. "Let's go!"

Nancy chuckled as Bess gazed longingly at the warm fire before saying, "I guess I'm as ready as

I'll ever be. I hope I don't turn into an icicle out there."

"You'll warm up in no time once you get moving," Matt assured her. The way he was looking at Bess, Nancy knew her friend would warm up in no time—from being with Matt, more than from skating.

They all grabbed their skates and made their way out the back door and down the long slope leading to the pond. Nancy was still lacing up her skates, sitting on one of the benches by the pond, when George slid onto the ice and began twirling in dizzying circles. Bess and Matt were the next ones on the ice, and they skated arm in arm. Tony, Nancy noticed, was less steady on his feet. He was wobbling a little as he made his way slowly around the pond.

"Hurry up, Nan, the ice is great!" George called.

"Ready!" She finished lacing up her skates and got up from the bench. Moving to the edge of the pond, she stepped out onto the ice. It was as smooth as glass. There were no twigs or dead leaves to mar it, and she remembered that Matt had gone home from the diner to sweep it especially for them.

She took a few tentative steps at first, then she was gliding in long, sure motions across the pond. Coming up next to Tony, she said, "Isn't this great?"

Tony gave her a weak smile. "I guess," he said.

He lurched forward unsteadily. "I was never very good at this."

"You must have had plenty of practice right here," Nancy said sweetly. "When you were a kid."

"Yeah, sure," he mumbled, but he wouldn't look at her.

Just then Matt and Bess whooshed up, laughing. "Come on, Tony," Matt said, "we'll tow you across the pond."

Tony started to protest, but Matt took one of his arms and Bess the other, and they skated off with Tony between them.

Nancy started doing easy jumps. She still wasn't sure what she thought about Matt or Tony, she realized as she curved around on the ice.

"Looking good, Nan," George said, breaking into Nancy's thoughts as she skated up. George's cheeks were red from the cold. She nodded her head toward Tony, who was still being held captive by Matt and Bess. "Maybe we should go rescue Tony. The poor guy."

Nancy laughed, but her voice was serious as she said, "I don't know if I feel so sorry for him. He's definitely hiding something."

"You mean about being such great friends with Matt?" George asked.

"Yeah. I mean, I was almost ready to think he wasn't the one who locked me in that room. He seemed really shocked. He acted completely natural at his office. I kind of liked him. But out here, around Matt, he's acting really strange."

George was skating in tiny circles in front of Nancy. "So maybe he *is* trying to steal Matt's money," she said. Digging the tip of one blade into the ice, she stopped to study Nancy with concerned eyes. "I'm not sure what to believe. But someone's afraid of you, Nan. You'd better be careful or you might really get hurt."

Suddenly Matt was in front of Nancy, making a dramatic, sweeping bow. "May I have your arm?" he asked, doffing his blue cap to her.

Had he overheard? Nancy had no way of knowing. Giving Matt her sweetest smile, she dropped him a curtsy and took his arm. Then they were off, gliding across the pond. They skated well together, and Nancy decided to take Bess's advice and just enjoy herself—for the moment.

As if reading her mind, Matt asked, "Having fun?" He grinned down at her and gave her arm a friendly squeeze.

"You bet," she said. And it was true. They didn't say anything for a few minutes, and Nancy let herself enjoy the crisp cold air and the smooth motions of the skating. Inevitably, the case crept back into her thoughts, though.

That article, for one thing. It was quite a coincidence that the person Matt interviewed turned out to be his father's ex-gardener. Nancy was about to ask him about it when someone yelled behind them.

Tony had fallen on the ice and was having a hard time getting back on his feet. Matt sped over and helped him to one of the benches to catch his breath. A moment later George had skated over to Nancy again.

"Do you think Matt heard what we were talking about?" she asked in a low voice.

Nancy shrugged. "I don't think so, but I'm not positive. I thought of something else, too, about that article. But I didn't have time to ask him about it." She looked over to where Matt, Bess, and Tony were sitting, then went on. "Why would the picture of Matt's father jog his memory about the past, when seeing Loomis in the flesh didn't? And why didn't Loomis recognize him?"

George shrugged. "I don't know—maybe Matt never really saw the gardener. They wouldn't necessarily have run into each other."

"I guess you're right," Nancy said, letting out a sigh. "I'm going to sit down for a minute. I need to clear my head."

Bess and Matt were just stepping back onto the ice as Nancy got off and sat down next to Tony on the bench.

"I should be going, Nancy," he said, bending over to unlace his skates. "Give my thanks to Mrs. Adams."

"Sure. Did you notice anything special about Matt?"

He glanced up and shook his head. "It's amazing," he began. "If I didn't know better—" He broke off his sentence, and suddenly he became extremely animated.

"There *is* something special, but I didn't think of it until now," he said. "Once when I was here, Matt had an accident."

"A serious one?"

"Not really." Tony pursed his mouth as he tried to remember. "Someone tripped him when he was skating, and he cut his wrist on a piece of sharp ice. It bled pretty badly. We were only about ten at the time."

Nancy looked at him, confused. "I'm not sure I see what the point is."

Tony's excitement continued. "The cut left a scar, that's the point. Right here." He pointed at his left wrist. "A half-moon shape. Check it out—see if it's there. I'll bet you it's not. And if it isn't, we have proof that this guy's a fake!"

"Hot chocolate," said George, grinning.

Bess chimed in, "And marshmallows, too! This is perfect, Mrs. Adams."

"If anything can un-numb my fingers, this is it," Nancy said, taking a mug from the beaming housekeeper.

The girls and Matt had left their skates and boots in the kitchen and were back in the library. Matt was reviving the embers of the fire, and they were all leaning on oversize pillows on the hearth rug.

"If you'd stayed out any longer, you'd have frozen to death," Mrs. Adams said, taking in their bright red cheeks. "Well, I'm off to bed." Matt kissed her cheek, and she blushed with pleasure.

Nancy had made a point of sitting next to Matt. She wanted to get a good look at his wrist. If Matt didn't have a scar—and if Tony was telling the truth—then Matt was a phony.

"I think my watch is fast," she said, shaking her wrist. "It says eleven forty-five, but it can't be that late."

Without hesitation, Matt hiked up the sleeve of his sweater and consulted the old-fashioned gold watch on his left wrist.

Nancy leaned over his shoulder. There was the scar, all right, exactly where Tony had told her it should be.

Before she could take a closer look, Matt shrugged the sleeve of his sweater back down and said, "What do you know. It really is a quarter to twelve." He shot one of his big grins across the room at Bess. "I was having so much fun with you guys that I lost track of the time."

Nancy rubbed her chin. Chalk up another piece of evidence in Matt's favor, she thought. Still, she wished she'd gotten a closer look. There was something . . .

"That's a neat watch you have, Matt," she said suddenly. "Do you mind if I take another look at it?"

"Sure." He pulled the sweater sleeve back up and said something about how the watch had belonged to his grandfather and Mrs. Adams had told him to wear it.

Nancy barely listened to his words, however. All of her attention was focused on the puckered skin that formed a half-moon on his wrist. She wasn't an expert on scars, but she was pretty sure that they faded to normal skin tone or paler with time.

But Matt's scar still was pinkish red—as if it was only a few months old—not ten or fifteen years!

Chapter

Nine

Hey, Nan, I could really get used to this, couldn't you?"

Bess's cheerful voice brought Nancy's attention back to the conversation in the library. Focusing on Bess and George, she saw that they had their stockinged feet stretched toward the glowing fire. Bess was munching on one of the sandwiches that had been left over from before they went skating.

Beside Nancy, Matt laughed and said to Bess, "You're welcome as often as you like." His blue eyes shone as he added, "And I hope it will be *very* often."

"It's really wonderful here," Nancy agreed, sipping her hot chocolate and checking out the glistening oak bookshelves and antique furniture. Inheriting Glover's Corners would definitely be worth an impostor having plastic surgery to give him a scar like the one the real Matt had had, Nancy added silently. She wished she knew for certain how old his scar was.

Nancy's brain was so full of *possible* scams. Maybe Matt was an impostor with a phony scar. Or maybe Tony was trying to cheat Matt out of his inheritance. Or maybe Mrs. Adams, or the ex-gardener Jake Loomis, was working with Matt. Her brain felt like a computer on overload —nothing would compute.

Boy, will I be relieved when tonight's over and I'm back home in bed, she thought. A good night's sleep is the only hope for me!

Over breakfast the next morning, Nancy told her father about the skating party and Matt's scar.

When she was done, Carson rubbed his chin thoughtfully. "The young man is taking a lie detector test down at city hall this morning," he said. "The test isn't always a hundred-percent reliable, but his willingness to take it is in his favor."

Nancy nodded. After her father had left to meet Matt, she poured herself a second glass of juice and sat back down at the kitchen table. Even after a good night's sleep, she wasn't sure where to start. She pulled out the article about

Loomis and began to reread it. Maybe there was something she had overlooked.

It wasn't until she was reading it for the fourth time that Nancy suddenly paused and drummed her fingers on the kitchen table. According to the article, Loomis Landscaping had its office in downtown Chicago. *Hmmm.* Matt might not have recognized Loomis during their interview a year ago, but had Loomis recognized *Matt?* It was a long shot, but she had to ask.

On an impulse, Nancy picked up the phone extension in the kitchen and called George. "Are you up for another trip to Chicago this morning?"

"Not another visit to the *Clarion?*" George's voice sounded skeptical.

"Nope. I want to talk to Jake Loomis this time."

"Good idea," George said. "Ready when you are, which, knowing you, is probably about ten minutes ago!"

Next, Nancy called Bess, but there wasn't any answer, so she headed out to her Mustang. It was as cold as ever outside, and the sky had a heavy, gray look to it.

"I hope it doesn't snow today," George said as she climbed into the car ten minutes later. "It looks as though the sky's going to open up and dump a huge pile of it on us."

Nancy shrugged. "That's fine with me—as

long as it holds off until we get back from Chicago."

"What's our story going to be?" George wanted to know as Nancy turned the Mustang toward the highway. "Are we still reporters?"

"I guess so. We'll say we're doing research for a *Who's Who in Chicago Business.*"

"Get him off his guard by buttering him up and making him feel important, eh?" George grinned. "Sounds good to me."

The traffic was heavy, but by midmorning they were in Chicago, and Nancy was winding her way through the crowded city streets to St. Paul Street, where the Loomis Landscaping office was. Luckily, she was able to park right outside.

"This is pretty familiar," Nancy said, getting her bearings before she and George went into the building. "If I'm not mistaken, the *Clarion* building is only a block east of here."

"Whatever you say." George grabbed her arm and pulled her toward the entrance. "It's a little cold for a geography lesson, Nan. Let's get inside."

In the marble-floored lobby, George let out an impressed whistle. "Not too shabby," she said in a low voice.

Nancy nodded her agreement. "It looks as if Jake Loomis has done pretty well for himself."

The office of Loomis Landscaping was a huge space that looked as if it had been converted from a warehouse. It was partitioned with low walls and tastefully decorated with plants and framed photos of colorful gardens. A blond woman sitting behind a wide reception desk asked the girls if she could help them.

"We'd like to see Mr. Loomis," Nancy said.

"Do you have an appointment?"

"No," said Nancy, "but we won't take much of his time." She gave her *Who's Who* spiel.

When she was done, the receptionist gave them a wide smile and said, "I'm sure Mr. Loomis won't mind giving you a few minutes." She picked up her phone and spoke into it briefly.

A moment later a man dressed in an expensive-looking suit emerged from a room at the far end of the office and headed toward them. He had salt-and-pepper hair with a beard to match and a burly, muscular build.

Jake Loomis received them with a big smile. Nancy and George followed him back to his office, which was large and furnished with a mahogany desk and leather-upholstered chairs.

"You girls look pretty young to be doing such important work," he said, gesturing for them to sit down in the leather chairs.

"We're older than we look," Nancy assured him, smiling. "Younger reporters do all the footwork, and the older ones get all the credit."

"Well, you can't have everything right away," he said. "Look at me. I didn't start to be successful until I was twice your age—at least." He spoke with a self-satisfied air, and Nancy suspected that he had probably made the same comment many times before.

George leaned forward and said, "We wanted to check up on something in the article about you in the *Clarion*—the one that came out about a year ago."

"Good article," Loomis said.

Ignoring his smug tone, Nancy went on. "It said that you had been a gardener for a private estate before you came to Chicago. Could you tell us whose estate it was?"

The smile left Loomis's craggy face, and he grunted. "What possible difference could it make?" he asked.

"It's important to know some background of the men and women we select for *Who's Who*," Nancy said, pressing him.

Jake Loomis rested his chin on his thick knuckles. "Oh, well," he said at last. "It can't matter now. The man is dead, quite recently, as a matter of fact. He won't know."

Nancy arched an eyebrow. "I'm sorry, I don't understand," she said.

"Let's just say we weren't exactly friends when I left. I quit after an argument with him. Glover was stubborn as a mule. That was his name, Clayton Glover. He was a hot-shot millionaire in River Heights." Loomis glowered at Nancy as he remembered, "The old man never would admit he was wrong. But I didn't want to make his life worse by mentioning him in that article."

Nancy pretended to take notes. She didn't understand why Loomis couldn't just mention Mr. Glover's name without bringing up whatever their fight had been about, but she didn't want to put him on the defensive.

"What do you mean, 'make his life worse'?" she asked.

Loomis shook his head. "You see, Glover was absolutely shattered after his only son died in an accident," he explained. "Matt was a great kid. I taught him everything he knew when he was small. I was more like a father to him than his own dad, if you know what I mean. The kid was only twelve or so when I left. I really missed him. Too bad his father and I couldn't see eye to eye."

Nancy nodded politely. She was curious as to what the argument had been about, but there was another important question she needed answered first. If Loomis had known Matt so well . . .

"You must have been happy to hear that Matt's alive," George said to Jake Loomis. "It's amazing, isn't it?"

Way to go, George! Nancy thought. You were reading my mind! She quickly added, "Yes, and it must have been a double surprise to you that Gary Page, the reporter who interviewed you, was really the long-lost Matt Glover." She watched Jake Loomis extra closely as she asked, "Did you recognize him at all when he interviewed you for the article?"

For a fraction of a second, Loomis just stared at Nancy and George. But then his heavyset face took on its smug expression again. "Yeah, well, I did notice the resemblance, but I didn't make much of it since I thought Matt was dead." Loomis let out a soft chuckle. "It sure was a surprise to see his picture in the paper, though."

"Oh, a lot of people were surprised, Mr. Loomis," George put in.

Loomis sat back in his chair and laughed out loud. "I'll bet. I understand a bunch of businesses have been waiting like vultures to get their hands on Glover's money. With Matt back, the hospital and the environmental people and the rest of them are all out of luck."

Nancy was about to ask Loomis if he'd tried to contact Matt at all since his return. She didn't have time to ask him any more questions, however, because just then the receptionist buzzed to announce another visitor.

"I'm sorry, girls, but I'm afraid I'll have to end our interview now," Loomis told them, getting up from his desk and showing Nancy and George to the office door. "When is this *Who's Who* coming out?" he asked.

"We'll let you know," George said hastily as they scooted out.

When they got outside, they saw that it had begun to snow. Nancy turned on the windshield wipers as they drove back to River Heights.

"What do you think?" George asked, popping

a tape in Nancy's newly repaired tape deck. "Was he telling us the truth?"

"I'm not sure, George. It certainly *could* be the truth," Nancy replied. "He didn't lie about who he'd worked for. But when he talked about Matt, I couldn't decide if he was telling the truth or not. I couldn't read him."

"Well, I didn't like him. He's too full of himself." George was tapping her foot to the beat of the music, but there was a frown on her face.

"Yeah," Nancy agreed. "And there's something else, too. He seemed to know an awful lot about the will, for someone who hasn't seen Matt or Mr. Glover in over ten years." She sighed. "But all that is supposing that Matt Glover is a phony. And if we're trying to find the most likely person to be an accomplice in a scam, I'd say Mrs. Adams wins. She'd know Matt better than anyone else."

George shook her head. "Oh, Nan, she's such a nice woman. I'd hate to think she's guilty of anything."

"So would I, but we can't rule out the possibility. I want to talk to her again.

"In fact, let's make a quick stop for some soup, then head over to Glover's Corners," Nancy suggested as she pulled up in front of her house.

The snow was falling very heavily and starting to accumulate by the time they set off for Glover's Corners. Switching on the weather report, the girls heard that more snow was expected.

Nancy drove very slowly and carefully. The snow was now almost a blanket of white against the front windshield, and she almost missed the gate to the Corners.

"I'm going to try to get a look at Mrs. Adams's room," Nancy said, creeping up the long, winding drive at a snail's pace.

"Where do I come in?" asked George.

"I need you to distract Mrs. Adams so I can search. If we're lucky, Matt's still with my father, taking that lie detector test."

"And how do I distract her?" George was staring at the ledges of snow being pushed off by the windshield wipers.

Nancy shrugged. "We'll just have to play it by ear, I guess."

Pulling to a stop in front of the house, she and George trudged through the snow to the front door. Nancy rang the bell and then heard it echoing somewhere deep in the old house.

"Listen," said George.

Nancy cocked her head to the side. She could hear Matt's voice, and it seemed to be coming from somewhere quite close. His tone sounded angry, although she couldn't distinguish his words.

Putting a finger to her lips, Nancy gestured to George to follow her. The snow cushioned the sound of their boots as they backed away from the door and moved toward the left wing of the house, where Matt's voice was coming from.

Walking almost to the screened-in porch at the end of the wing, Nancy could make out Matt standing on the porch. Despite the cold, he was wearing only a button-down shirt and jeans, and he was talking on a cordless phone.

"Nancy! George! What are you doing here?"

The two girls jumped in surprise and saw Bess leaning out a living room window.

Nancy gasped, knowing that Matt must have heard, too.

When she looked back to the porch, she saw that Matt had stopped talking into the cordless phone—and was now staring at her with cold, unwelcoming eyes.

Chapter

Ten

NANCY GAVE MATT a tentative smile and waved at him. Instantly an answering smile spread across his face, making her wonder if she'd just been imagining his angry scowl.

"It's freezing out there," Bess called to Nancy and George as they made their way back to the front door. "Hurry up and come in!"

As the girls brushed the snow off themselves and stepped inside, Bess asked again, "What are you guys doing here?"

"I guess we could ask you the same question," said George.

Bess spoke in an excited rush as she explained. "I ran into Matt downtown at the bakery. He was buying a cake for Mrs. Adams. It's some kind of tradition they have or something. Anyway, he suggested I come back and share it. I thought it would be rude to say no."

"So you were just being polite, eh?" said George, rolling her eyes. "I don't suppose that the opportunity to spend time with the super-gorgeous Matt Glover had anything to do with your decision?"

"Absolutely not," said Bess indignantly. Then she blushed. "Well, maybe a little. I mean, I know he's not going to fall in love with me or anything, but I just think he's so *romantic!*

"Now it looks like we're getting snowed in," Bess went on. From the flushed look on her face, Nancy could tell that being snowed in with Matt Glover would be Bess's idea of paradise.

Nancy couldn't help smiling at Bess. It was great that she was so happy. Nancy just hoped she wouldn't be disappointed.

"I hope we're not ruining your romantic afternoon," Nancy said apologetically. "We really came to see Mrs. Adams."

"I'm glad you're here." Bess looked around. "Matt must still be on the phone. I guess we can just go to the kitchen."

As they walked down the hall, Bess turned to George and Nancy and said, "Oh, by the way, it so happens that Matt passed the lie-detector test with flying colors. I think you owe him an apology, both of you."

Nancy was surprised. "Did Matt tell you himself that he passed?" she asked. If so, there was a chance he was lying.

"Nope. Your father did. I saw him just as he was leaving his office, before I ran into Matt."

"Lie-detector tests aren't infallible," Nancy said, "but passing is definitely a good sign for Matt." If Matt was an impostor, she would have expected the lie-detector results to be inconclusive at best.

Bess frowned. "'A good sign'? That's all? You're such a skeptic, Nan. When are you going to admit that Matt Glover really is back?"

"When all the evidence is in," Nancy said, pushing through the door to the kitchen.

Mrs. Adams was sitting at the long oak table. Nancy was surprised to see that her eyes were red, as if she had been crying. She was staring out the kitchen window and didn't even seem to notice that the three girls had come in.

"Anything wrong, Mrs. Adams?" George asked gently.

The housekeeper jumped half out of her seat, then relaxed when she saw Nancy, George, and Bess. "Oh, I am jumpy lately, aren't I?" she said, smiling wanly. "I—I suppose it's all this excitement, what with Matt coming home so suddenly."

Nancy wondered if Mrs. Adams had heard that Matt had passed the lie-detector test. If so, she didn't seem very happy about it. In fact, she seemed more depressed than Nancy had seen her since Mr. Glover's funeral.

"Isn't it great news about the lie-detector test?" Nancy said, taking a seat beside the housekeeper at the table. Bess and George sat down opposite.

"Yes, yes," Mrs. Adams said halfheartedly. "Wonderful news." She heaved a deep sigh, then rose with effort and went to cut slices from a chocolate cake that sat on the silver server where the pie had been the night before.

"Would you girls like a slice of this lovely cake?" she asked. Her voice sounded even more distraught to Nancy, and there were tears in her eyes now. "Matt was good enough to bring it home from the bakery."

"No, thanks," Nancy said. "Maybe later."

"Speak for yourself, Nan," George put in. "I'd love a piece."

"Me, too," Bess chimed in. In response to her cousin's questioning look, she said, "The first piece I had wasn't very big."

Nancy and George chuckled, but Nancy noticed that Mrs. Adams didn't even crack a smile as she expertly cut slices for George and Bess, slid them onto two plates, and passed them over. The housekeeper's hands were trembling.

Nancy was about to ask Mrs. Adams what was wrong but stopped herself when she heard Matt's voice, just outside the kitchen.

"Hey, everyone," he was calling. "The radio says this is a blizzard!"

Matt entered the kitchen like a comet and turned a big smile on Nancy and George. "I'm so glad you're both here," he said, his voice bubbling with enthusiasm. "I was thinking we could go for a sleigh ride."

"But there aren't horses at Glover's Corners anymore," George pointed out between bites of chocolate cake. The estate stables had once held two or three horses, but after Matt's disappearance Mr. Glover had sold them off, Nancy remembered.

"There's a stable a short walk from here, though," Matt said. "Thurston's. They rent sleighs along with the horses. I just called to check it out. Come on, now. You have to come— it's all set up."

"In a blizzard?" Bess inquired nervously.

"It's supposed to let up before long," answered Matt. "And we have plenty of spare scarves and gloves and stuff to bundle up with."

Bess still looked dubious, but she said, "Well, okay."

"Let's do it!" said George.

"It'll be fun," Nancy agreed. She was glad for a chance to see more of Matt. When they came back, maybe she'd be able to check out Mrs. Adams's room and find out if what was bothering her had anything to do with Matt.

"Great. I better get to the stable before we're

completely snowed in." Before he left the kitchen, Matt looked over at Mrs. Adams. "Have a piece of cake, Addie," he said warmly. "I got it especially for you."

Mrs. Adams began to cry as soon as Matt left the room. Nancy put one arm around her shoulders. "What is it, Mrs. Adams?" she asked.

The housekeeper reached for a paper napkin and rubbed at her eyes. "It's really nothing, dear, nothing for you to worry about. I have the most terrible headache—it just won't go away."

"Can I get you some aspirin?" George offered.

Mrs. Adams shook her head. "No, thank you, dear. I think I'll just lie down for a while."

"I'll help you to your room," Nancy said.

"I don't know what's the matter with me," Mrs. Adams said as Nancy led her up the stairs. "I should be so happy, under the circumstances. . . ." Her voice trailed off.

Nancy wanted to find out what was upsetting Mrs. Adams, but she was afraid any questions would only upset her more. Nancy kept her arm firmly around the older woman's shoulders until they reached her third-floor room.

It was large and comfortable—everything was neat as a pin. The windows had a gorgeous view of the back garden and the pond, even though it was distorted by the thick sheets of heavily falling snow.

Mrs. Adams sat on the edge of her bed and let her head fall into her hands. Moving over to her,

Nancy noticed that there were three photographs on the bedside table. One was of Matt as a little boy, sitting on a pony. Another was of Clayton Glover, and the third was of Mrs. Adams and Matt sitting side by side on one of the benches that circled the pond.

She knew she shouldn't let her emotions get in the way of the case, but she just couldn't imagine that Mrs. Adams would do anything to deceive the Glover family, even after Mr. Glover's death. Obviously, they had been the most important people in her life.

Gently, Nancy helped Mrs. Adams to lie back on the bed, then went back downstairs. She paused at the landing to phone home to let her father and Hannah know that they were all waiting out the storm at Glover's Corners.

Nancy found Bess and George in the library. George was feeding pine cones to the fire, while Bess was lazily flipping through the pages of a magazine. Nancy picked up a magazine to look at, too.

"How's Mrs. Adams?" Bess asked at last, putting her magazine down.

Nancy plopped down on the sofa beside her. "Resting. I'm sure she'll feel better in a while."

"She's had a lot to deal with, what with Matt coming back and all," Bess said sympathetically.

"If it really is Matt," George added quietly.

"I'm sorry, Bess," she said in response to the

dark look her cousin shot her, "but you've got to be prepared for that possibility."

"I just know it's Matt," Bess insisted. "I would be able to tell if it weren't." She was about to say something else, but paused before going on excitedly, "Listen—the sleighs!"

They all rushed to a window. The storm had begun to let up, and Nancy could see that fresh snow lay deep and thick around Glover's Corners and in the woods beyond. The sun was low on the horizon, and the sleighs and snow all had a pinkish glow to them.

"There's Matt!" Bess exclaimed, pointing to a figure in an Eskimo-style parka driving the first sleigh.

"That must be someone from Thurston's stables in the other sleigh," said George.

Bringing up the rear was a four-wheel-drive Land Rover—the only kind of vehicle that could make it through the snow before the plows came.

"I wonder why he rented two of them?" Nancy asked. "One is big enough for the four of us."

George was already heading for the front closet, where their jackets and boots were. "Who cares why? It'll be so much fun. Let's go!"

They struggled into the warmest clothes they could find in the cloakroom. Bess wound a long, fluffy, red muffler around her neck and picked up a pair of matching mittens. "Hey, Nan," she said, pointing to a bright blue woolen hat hanging from a peg, "you should wear that. It'll look fantastic with your hair."

Nancy's hat was still wet so she pulled on the cap, then the girls went outside. As they tromped through the snow to the sleighs, the man who had driven the second sleigh was climbing into the Land Rover. "We'll be back in an hour," Nancy heard him tell Matt. "Enjoy your ride."

Matt's face was glowing from the cold. "Hey, my hat looks good on you," he complimented Nancy.

For a second Bess looked the tiniest bit jealous of the compliment, but at Matt's next words her face lit up. "I thought Bess and I would take one sleigh and you two the other," he said to Nancy and George. "You do know how to drive?" he asked Nancy. She nodded.

"We'll follow the old trails through the woods and meet back here in an hour if we split up."

"Terrific!" said Bess, hopping up next to Matt in the first sleigh.

As Nancy and George climbed into the second sleigh, George commented in an undertone, "Bess's nervousness sure disappeared in a hurry."

"I'll say," Nancy agreed, pulling the heavy lap robe over their knees. "Her crush on Matt is getting even bigger. I just wish she'd back off a little until we're sure about him."

Nancy watched as Matt and Bess led the way,

starting out for the woods. Taking the reins, she urged their horse to follow.

There seemed to be no sounds in the world but the jangling sleigh bells, the creak of leather, and the snorts of the horses as they went forward in the snow.

"This is great." George sighed. "I'd forgotten how wonderful a sleigh ride can be."

"It *is* beautiful," Nancy agreed.

Soon they were deep in the woods, with its mixture of tall pines and sturdy oaks. The sun was very low now, and deep shadows had settled around the tree trunks, but the snow still shone with a beautiful, pearly glow. Nancy felt herself relaxing as she followed Matt and Bess's sleigh, which was about twenty yards ahead of them.

Seeing Matt's sleigh veer off onto a narrower path to the left, Nancy said, "I guess we should follow." She began to maneuver their horse to turn left. "I don't want to get lost out here."

The path was just wide enough for the sleigh, and lined by trees on both sides. Their horse was moving at a good trot now, and the tree branches seemed to whiz by them. Nancy had to concentrate to see clearly through the thick shadows.

Suddenly she started. At first she just saw a blur, then she realized it was someone in a red hunting jacket stepping out from beneath the pines, right into the path of her sleigh!

Instinctively, she gripped the reins hard and

pulled back, but she could see the sleigh was moving too fast to stop in time. "Hey! Get out of the way!" she yelled, but the figure in red hurtled onto the path directly in front of them and streaked by under the horse's startled nose.

"Watch out!" George shouted.

The horse reared in panic, and Nancy gripped the reins harder. Then she felt them snap in two in her hands. She watched in horror as the leather strips slid from her grasp and dropped behind the wild horse, leaving her with two useless ends. A second later the horse bolted and took off into the woods.

The horse was still attached to the sleigh by the traces, but there was no way to control the animal. The sleigh teetered and then went careening after the horse, into the woods and down a slope. Tree branches whipped at Nancy's face, and the forest went by in a blinding blur.

"We're going to go over!" she heard George yell beside her.

The last thing Nancy saw was a huge oak rushing toward her. Then everything went black.

Chapter

Eleven

WHEN NANCY OPENED her eyes again, the first thing she saw was Mrs. Adams's worried face floating above her.

Nancy's head was pounding, but when she gingerly moved her legs, then her arms, she found that they worked. Turning her head, she looked around, squinting, and saw she was lying under a goose-down quilt in a bedroom at Glover's Corners.

"What?" she began, but Mrs. Adams put a finger to her lips and said a doctor was on the way.

Nancy looked over Mrs. Adams's shoulder at the snow-covered tree branches outside the bedroom window. She blinked, dimly remembering the runaway sleigh, the startled horse, and the oak tree. There was something else, too, but her mind felt so foggy she couldn't concentrate on it.

Letting out a sigh, she shut her eyes again. That was when it came to her—the figure in red hurtling across the path in front of them. Someone had deliberately frightened the horse. But who?

Nancy felt a cool, soothing cloth being placed on her forehead. Opening her eyes again, she asked Mrs. Adams, "Is George all right?"

"George landed in a snowbank. She's fine."

Nancy tried to tell the housekeeper that someone had startled her horse on purpose, but Mrs. Adams told her not to talk until the doctor had examined her. Nancy stared at the ceiling, trying to get her thoughts together. Her head felt woozy. She could hear the muted voices of George, Bess, and Matt from somewhere beyond the bedroom door. The sound was lulling and comforting.

She must have drifted off, because when she opened her eyes again a kind-looking man was sitting by her bed. Mrs. Adams introduced him as Dr. Biddle. This time Nancy felt wide-awake and clearheaded. She greeted the doctor with: "I'm really fine—you shouldn't have bothered to come out on my account."

"Now, hush, young lady," the doctor told her with a smile. He examined her eyes with a little penlight and asked her if she was feeling dizzy.

Nancy shook her head. "I just have a king-size headache."

"It's no wonder," Dr. Biddle told her. "You must have the hardest head in River Heights, to have gotten the better of that tree you ran into. If you had a concussion it was a very minor one. I don't think X rays will be needed."

After the doctor left, Nancy took some aspirin. When the pounding in her head had lessened a little, she went downstairs to the library. Matt was standing on the hearth by the fire, and Bess and George were sitting on the couch. They all looked worried. Matt rushed over to Nancy when she stepped into the room.

"Nancy, are you all right?" he asked. "You really gave us a scare back there." He led her over to a chair beside Bess and George and poured her a steaming cup of tea from a china tea service on the table in front of the couch.

"Someone gave my *horse* a scare," Nancy replied evenly. She took a sip of the tea. "Mmmm, this tastes good. I'm starting to feel better."

Bess looked up, her blue eyes filled with concern. "That's awful. You guys could have gotten killed, and Matt and I didn't even know anything was wrong until George screamed for us."

"You wouldn't have seen anything, unless you were looking back," Nancy said. "A person dressed in a red jacket ran out from the trees right in front of us."

Matt nodded. "That's what George said. Did you see who it was?"

"No, and I don't even know if it was a man or a woman. It all happened so fast."

"I do remember one thing," George said, leaning back against the plush pillows of the couch. "Whoever it was had a ski cap pulled low so it was impossible to see the face clearly."

"I don't suppose it could have been an accident?" Bess asked.

"Oh, come off it, Bess," George told her cousin. "People don't wait around in the woods in a snowstorm and charge out in front of a horse by accident. Whoever did it meant for Nancy or me to get badly hurt, maybe even killed. And somehow I don't think whoever it was was after me."

Matt looked troubled. "If someone is trying to hurt Nancy, it must be because of me—because of the investigation she's been doing to see if I'm who I say I am." He held up a hand as Nancy started to speak. "Yes, I know you haven't been sure about me. I heard Bess telling you about the lie-detector results earlier. I do understand your suspicion, believe me. I know it's a strange story to swallow, but I hope soon you'll believe I'm telling the truth about who I am."

Watching Matt as he paced back and forth in front of the fire, his blue eyes earnest and troubled, Nancy was almost positive he was telling the truth.

"What we have to think about is who could

have done such a thing," Matt went on. He paused to look at Nancy. "Do you have any suspicions?"

Nancy shook her head, waiting for him to speak. He stopped his pacing as if he had an idea.

"I hate to say it," Matt said at last, "but it must be one of the people who would have inherited my father's fortune if I hadn't reappeared. Like maybe Tony Giralda."

So Matt had thought of that possibility, too, Nancy thought with a touch of admiration.

"You could be right," she told him. "There's something else we should consider, too. I don't think the attacker was necessarily after me. It's just as likely that the person was trying to get *you* out of the way, Matt, so that your father's money would be distributed to the causes named in the will."

Bess gasped. "Oh, no!" she wailed.

"That makes sense," said George. "Whoever it was could have mistaken our sled for Matt's. It was pretty shadowy out there, so it would have been hard to tell who was in which sled."

"I'll bet it *was* Tony Giralda," Bess said emphatically. "He's so intense!"

"His work is his whole life," Matt pointed out. "If he loses it, he loses everything. He's barely surviving as it is. He needs that money."

Matt came over and knelt in front of Nancy's chair. He put a hand on her shoulder and stared into her eyes. "I'm sorry that I've caused you so much trouble. If anything happened to you because of me I'd—I don't know what I'd do."

Nancy studied Matt's blue eyes carefully, but there was nothing in them but sincere concern. "Thank you, Matt," she said.

As Matt went over to put another log on the fire, Mrs. Adams came in with fresh tea. She smiled at them, but Nancy saw that the housekeeper still had a pained look on her face, and her step had lost its usual energetic bounce.

As she bent to place the fresh teapot on the table, she leaned close to Nancy and whispered very softly, "I have something to tell you."

Nancy blinked, surprised. Obviously Mrs. Adams wanted to talk with her in private. Getting to her feet, Nancy picked up the tray with the cold teapot on it and said, "Here, Mrs. Adams, I'll help you clear this."

In the kitchen Mrs. Adams didn't waste any time telling Nancy what was bothering her.

"There's something I want you to know," the woman began. She leaned over the counter and began chopping carrots and tossing them in a big stewing pot. "Ordinarily I'd wait until you were feeling better, but this can't wait."

"I'm fine, don't worry about me," Nancy reassured her. There were some stalks of celery on the counter, too, and Nancy went to work on them, chopping and tossing them into the pot.

"When you came into the kitchen earlier to-

day, I suppose you could see I'd been crying."
Mrs. Adams sniffled, and Nancy waited quietly
until she continued.

"I was so happy when Matt came home. It
seemed like a dream come true. But now—now I
don't know what to believe, Nancy." She lowered
her voice to a whisper. "I don't trust him anymore."

Nancy looked curiously at Mrs. Adams. "I'm
sorry, but I'm not sure I understand," she said.
"Why don't you trust him?"

Mrs. Adams took a deep breath. "You know
how it is when you want to believe something so
badly, you overlook all sorts of things in order to
convince yourself?"

"Sure," said Nancy.

"Well, it wasn't like that at all with me," Mrs.
Adams said defiantly. "I didn't have to overlook
signs that Matt wasn't my Matt, because there
simply weren't any. Everything he did, everything he said, was exactly what I expected of the
Matt I remember. He even remembered to bring
me a cake today, when he had so much on his
mind."

She pressed her hands to her mouth to stop the
trembling of her lips. "You see, it was a custom in
this house, way back when Matt was little. I
would bake a pie, or a cake, and when it was
finished, Mr. Glover would bring us a new one
from the bakery."

"What a nice way to show his appreciation of you," Nancy said, reaching for another celery stalk.

Mrs. Adams wiped away a tear with her finger. "That's what Mr. Glover said, that I deserved to be spoiled, the way I looked after them. Made me feel like one of the family. I told him I loved baking, but he insisted. He was such a considerate man. And now that he's gone, Matt is continuing the tradition."

"I'm sorry, Mrs. Adams, but I don't quite see what you're leading up to," Nancy said, a puzzled frown on her face.

The housekeeper looked at Nancy with anguished eyes. "The cake," she said. "It was—"

"Nan, your father's on the phone." Bess had come into the kitchen. "Need any help, Mrs. Adams?" She crossed the room and took the knife Nancy had put down on the counter. "I'll give you a hand while Nancy talks to him."

Nancy assured her father that she was all right and said she'd be home as soon as the snowplows cleared the road. When she returned to the kitchen, however, she saw that George and Matt had joined Bess and Mrs. Adams there, and they seemed prepared to stay for a while.

So much for learning Mrs. Adams's secret about Matt, Nancy thought, frustrated. She didn't have a chance to get Mrs. Adams alone again until after they'd eaten a dinner of beef stew and salad, and finished up the chocolate cake.

"That was delicious," Bess said, pushing her empty plate away from her. "I couldn't eat another bite."

George shot her cousin a teasing look and said, "That's good, because I doubt there's another bite left after those two servings of everything you ate."

"How about watching a tape on the VCR," Matt suggested, getting up from the table. "My dad had a pretty good selection of old movies. They're in the den."

As the others followed him toward the den, Nancy stayed behind to help Mrs. Adams clear the table.

"What were you saying before about the chocolate cake?" she asked the housekeeper, picking up the conversation they'd started earlier.

"It was chocolate," Mrs. Adams said.

Nancy stared at her. "Is there something strange about that?"

Fresh tears sprang to Mrs. Adams's eyes as she explained in a quiet voice, "It's anything chocolate. I'm terribly allergic to it. The one kind of cake Matt Glover would never bring me is the one he brought today."

Nancy thought for a moment. "Is it possible that he's forgotten?" she suggested. "After all these years, maybe—"

"He'd remember this," Mrs. Adams interrupted. "It's a very severe allergy. When he was a little boy, I ate something with chocolate in it by mistake. My throat swelled up, and I could hardly breathe. Mr. Glover had to send for the doctor. It scared Matt half to death, I remember."

Nancy nodded. "You're right, he wouldn't be likely to forget anything as dramatic as that."

"That's why I don't think that boy is Matt Glover. It breaks my heart to say so, but he's not Matt."

Mrs. Adams's words were still ringing in Nancy's ears when she joined the others in the den. She could hardly concentrate on the movie —some spy thriller about a Russian double agent. She kept stealing glances at Matt, who was sitting next to Bess on the couch and acting as charming and natural as ever.

When the movie was over, Nancy glanced out the den window and was relieved to see that a plow had come to clear the driveway. That must mean the roads had been plowed, too. Her head had started to pound again, and all she could think about was going home and getting into bed. While Bess and Matt rewound the video, Nancy and George went out to the front closet.

"I'm exhausted," said Nancy, opening the closet door. She pulled her jacket off its hanger and pushed aside some other coats to get to

George's. That was when she saw it—a flash of red peeking out from beneath some raincoats.

Her heart pounded in her chest as she pulled the raincoats aside. An old red hunting jacket hung on a peg near the back of the closet. Reaching out, she fingered the sleeve. It was slightly damp.

"George!" she gasped. "It's the red hunting jacket! The one the person wore to spook our horse!"

"You're right!" George exclaimed, peering into the closet over Nancy's shoulder. "But what's it doing here?"

"Whoever scared our horse put it here."

George frowned. "But we're the only ones around here, and none of us was wearing it, because we were all *in* the sleighs."

Nancy's voice dropped to a whisper as she said, "Not *all* of us. There was one other person around—someone who wasn't in the sleighs, someone who knew that we were." She paused. "Rosemary Adams."

Chapter
Twelve

GEORGE STARED AGAIN at the red hunting jacket. "Nan, do you really think a sixty-year-old woman would go tromping out in knee-deep snow to try to kill someone?" she asked doubtfully.

"It does seem pretty unlikely," Nancy replied, smiling at the ridiculous picture George's words painted in her mind. But her face swiftly grew grim again as another point occurred to her.

"George, this case just gets more complicated the more I get into it," she complained. She told her friend what Mrs. Adams had said about Matt bringing home the chocolate cake.

"So Mrs. Adams doesn't think that guy is really Matt Glover," George summarized when Nancy was done.

"Right, and there's something else. Remember I was wearing Matt's blue wool hat on the ride?"

"Yeah. So?" George prompted.

"So I looked like Matt," Nancy said excitedly. "Don't you see? That makes it even more likely that whoever spooked our horse expected to get Matt's sleigh. Especially if that person was someone who would recognize that cap as Matt's. Someone like Mrs. Adams."

"You're saying that Mrs. Adams spooked our horse in an effort to kill Matt? Why? Because she was angry at him for being a phony?" George's brown eyes were skeptical. "Sorry, Nancy. I don't buy that."

"I know it sounds far out, but it is possible," Nancy said. She snapped her fingers as she remembered something else. "Or if you don't like that, try this one on for size. Matt was wearing that blue cap the night we went skating —and Tony Giralda was there."

"Hey, I like that better," George said. "He does have a big reason for wanting Matt out of the way. But if it was Tony, how'd he get hold of this jacket?"

Nancy pulled out George's coat and handed it to her. "Well, when we left the house for the sleigh ride, Mrs. Adams was resting in her room. He could have come in while she was upstairs, taken one of the old jackets, and replaced it after causing our accident." Then her face fell. "Actually," she said, crestfallen, "just about anyone could have done that."

"Not quite anyone," George put in. "Even if Matt is a phony, the way Mrs. Adams says, he couldn't have done it."

"No, he's in the clear since he was in the other sleigh with Bess," Nancy agreed. "Anyway, I'm not sure the chocolate cake business is enough to prove that this Matt is an impostor. Sure, it would be frightening for a child to see someone having a violent allergic reaction, but Matt wouldn't necessarily remember that it was caused by chocolate. After all, Mrs. Adams still made hot chocolate for Matt and the other kids, didn't she? It wasn't as if the whole household was deprived of chocolate just because their housekeeper was allergic to it."

"Now, *that* would be something you'd remember," George put in, grinning. "Amnesia or not."

Nancy laughed, but her voice was serious when she said, "On the other hand, Matt's new-looking scar *is* kind of suspicious, and—" She snapped her fingers.

"What is it, Drew?" George said. "I know that look, and it usually means you're about to get us into some crazy situation."

"Not this time," Nancy said, laughing. "But it just occurred to me: What if Matt hired two sleighs because he *knew* something was going to happen—because he planned it! It's possible."

"In that case, it would have to have been Matt's accomplice." George sighed. "Who do we think that is?" she asked plaintively. "I'm so confused!"

"The most likely person to be Matt's accomplice is Jake Loomis," Nancy reminded George. "I think we can rule out Mrs. Adams on that score, since she's now claiming that Matt isn't really Matt—if you know what I mean."

George groaned. "I guess so." She peered down the hallway. "I keep expecting Bess and Matt to come out of the den. They're really taking a long time to rewind that video, don't you think?"

At that moment Bess and Matt appeared. Bess's face was suffused with happiness. After they had said goodbye and the girls had climbed into the car, she said in a dreamy voice, "You guys, Matt asked me to go to the movies this weekend. I'm beginning to think I really might have a chance with him."

"Bess, he's much older than you," George objected. "Get real!"

Nancy didn't say anything, but she made a silent vow: one way or another, she was going to have this case solved by the weekend. She couldn't sit by not knowing the truth—not when her friend's happiness might be at stake.

Half an hour later Nancy pulled up in front of Tony Giralda's Environmental Action office. Her mind was racing after finding the red jacket, and she felt too agitated to just go home.

During the drive she had made a mental list of the three suspects for the accident with the sleigh. The first, Mrs. Adams, might have done it hoping to scare or hurt Matt, whom she believed to be a phony. Nancy knew that possibility was slim, so she set it aside. She'd check out the others first.

She had to consider both Giralda and Jake Loomis as likely suspects; Tony because he wanted to get Matt out of the way, Loomis because—if Matt was a phony, and he was Matt's accomplice—he wanted to get Nancy off the case. Anyway, the sooner Nancy checked these two out, the better.

Good, he was working late. The lights were still on, Nancy thought as she parked in front of Tony's office. The fresh snow was up to the tops of her boots as she made her way to the front door. Finding it unlocked, she let herself in quietly. She was about to call out when she heard Tony's voice. It sounded as if he was on the telephone.

"I'm sorry, ma'am," he was saying. "I know I'm a little late with the rent, but if you can just wait a few more days I'll—Yes, I know, but—"

Nancy listened attentively. It was obvious that Tony was having money troubles.

Silence. Then, "Please believe me. I'm expecting some donations this week. It's not a case of being desperate, it's—" His voice took on an angry tone. "Look, this is a small operation. I'm practically waging a one-man war against pollution in our river—"

The person on the other end of the line kept cutting Tony off, so Nancy didn't hear much more of his side of the conversation. At last he put down the phone.

Nancy called out to let Tony know she was there.

He was frowning as he came through the doorway to the hall, but when he saw Nancy, his expression lightened. "What a nice surprise," he told her. "I was expecting a lady with an eviction notice, and I get Nancy Drew instead. What brings you here tonight?"

Tony beckoned Nancy into his office. Nancy hesitated when she saw Fred lying next to the desk chair, but the big dog's tail began to wag when he saw her so she sat down tentatively.

"I couldn't help but overhear," she began.

Tony shook his head and told her, "Some people don't understand that it's a struggle to make ends meet around here. They act as if my Environmental Action was funded by the Rockefeller Foundation or something." He sighed. "I mean, I work day and night. People like my landlady don't realize how tough it is."

But it would be a lot easier if Matt Glover turns out to be an impostor and you get some of Mr. Glover's money, Nancy thought. Clearing her throat, she said, "Do you mind if I ask where you were this afternoon between, say, five and six o'clock?"

"Right here, where I always am," Tony replied. "What's this about?" he asked irritably.

The look on his face darkened as Nancy explained, and finally he blurted out, "Look, if anything's happened, it was caused by that jerk who's calling himself Matt Glover. Didn't you check out his scar?"

Nancy nodded. "He has a scar, but it looks kind of fresh—maybe too new to have been gotten when he was a kid. I couldn't tell, though."

She took a deep breath. "I'd like to trust you, Tony, but you're not being totally open with me. There's something you've never mentioned."

Tony glowered at her as he raked a hand through his blond hair. "Yeah? What's that?"

"Clayton Glover's money," Nancy said.

He put up his hands in a gesture of helplessness. "I won't deny that I'll miss the money. Mr. Glover used to make a donation to me every year, but what can I do? He can't give from beyond the grave, can he?"

"I didn't mean his donations, Tony. I meant big money, enough to let you run this place in style."

"Where's that supposed to come from?" he asked, giving her a skeptical look.

Leaning forward, she told him, "Giralda's

Environmental Action is in Mr. Glover's will. It was one of the charities he provided for. Because of Matt's reappearance, you stand to lose a lot, Tony. Obviously your interest in proving him to be an impostor goes beyond just a 'gut feeling.'"

Tony's jaw hung open in disbelief. "And you thought I *knew* that?" he asked. "I had no idea!"

His reaction was so shocked that Nancy had a hard time thinking he could be lying. But she was puzzled. "If that's true, then why is it so important to you to expose Matt? I mean, could you really have known him well enough to be so convinced he's a phony?" She shot him a sarcastic look and added, "I think we can drop the idea that you knew him like a brother."

Tony flushed. "Okay, maybe I stretched the truth a little when I said that Matt and I were really tight, but only because I thought you wouldn't take me seriously otherwise."

He took a deep breath before continuing. "I wasn't part of his circle of close friends or anything. They were pretty elite, and I didn't feel comfortable around them. But Matt was a regular guy. He was always really nice to me—not stuck up at all. We used to talk a lot at school, and he did invite me out to the Corners a few times." He smiled sheepishly. "Not as much as I made it sound, though."

"But you still think you knew him well enough to know that this Matt is a fake?" Nancy asked.

"It's just a feeling I have. Maybe it's because I'm a guy and I'm not distracted by his good looks."

Nancy ignored his annoying comment. "Look, Tony," she told him, "I promise you I'll expose Matt if he isn't who he claims to be."

Nancy got up to leave, and Tony walked her to her car. "So Mr. Glover really left me something in his will, huh?" He looked both proud and surprised. "That was pretty decent of him."

After saying good night, Nancy drove back toward her house. Could she scratch Tony off her list of suspects? He claimed he hadn't even known he had anything to gain from Mr. Glover's will. But he could have found out—the provisions of the will seemed to be common knowledge to other people.

Nancy rubbed her temples. Her head was still aching, and she was ready to get some sleep.

"Talk about long days," she said to her father as she entered the house. "Today was a killer."

Carson Drew was sitting in the living room, reading. He looked up at her with concern. "You almost *did* get killed," he reminded her. "Promise me you'll be careful, Nancy."

"Dad, you know I always am." She sat down on the sofa next to him. "Bess told me Matt passed the lie-detector test."

Her father held out the sheets of paper he'd been reading. "Yes," he said. "In fact I was just looking it over more closely. I want to make sure of the results before we wrap this up."

"And?" Nancy looked at him expectantly.

"Matt did extremely well. The important things checked out in his favor. The test shows he's telling the truth when he says that he is Matthew Glover, that he was born in River Heights, that he is the son of Clayton Glover—essential things like that."

"Was there anything that *didn't* check out?"

"Only one thing. We asked him the same question several times, and he always answered yes. But the machine went haywire, indicating that he might not have been telling the truth."

Nancy looked at her father. "What was the question?"

"It was," said Carson Drew, " 'Have you ever been in Colorado?' "

"You're kidding!" Nancy exclaimed. "But the real Matt would have to have known he'd been in Colorado. That's where he was lost in the avalanche!"

Chapter

Thirteen

Nancy stared at her father. "If Matt was lying about being in Colorado," she said slowly, thinking out loud, "he must have been lying about all the other stuff, too." She paused, frowning. "But the test showed that he was telling the truth. Why?"

Carson held up his hands. "These tests aren't always reliable," he said. "There can be all sorts of inconsistencies."

Nancy yawned, then rubbed her head, which was still throbbing. "Well, I won't be able to think straight until I get a good night's sleep." She said good night, then went up to her room, dropping off almost as soon as her head hit the pillow.

The following morning she woke up with only a ghost of her headache. Her first thought as she sat up in bed was about the way the reins had felt as they snapped apart in her hands right before the accident.

She blinked as the thought struck her—reins didn't simply rip in two. A stable that rented horses and sleighs couldn't afford to let their leather get so dried out that their clients were in danger.

"Somebody tampered with them," she said aloud. Jumping out of bed, she dressed quickly in jeans, a white turtleneck, and a blue sweater. After eating a bowl of cereal and gulping down some juice, Nancy grabbed a jacket and went out to her car. "First stop, Thurston's livery stables," she said.

The sun reflected off the fields of dazzling snow in a blinding glare, and Nancy had to squint to see as she drove to the stables, a few miles outside of River Heights. She turned into the entrance, marked by a sign in the shape of a huge horse's head. It read: "Thurston's Livery—Horses for Hire, Sleigh Rides in Season."

Nancy parked in a lot in front of a big red barn that had that same horse's head and motto painted on it. A wooden shack jutted out from the barn on one side of the entrance, and Nancy went over to it.

She knocked on the door, and a young man

with ruddy cheeks opened it and gestured for her to enter. He introduced himself as Charlie Murphy.

"What can I do for you?" he asked, all smiles.

Inside, the pungent odor of horses and hay struck Nancy immediately. A rear door in the shack opened into the barn, and Nancy caught a glimpse of stalls against one wall.

"I just wanted to check on something," Nancy said, returning Charlie's smile. "When things like reins get old, and the leather becomes thin, is there a way to mend them?"

"Mend them?" Charlie's smile faded. He pulled out a chair for her and perched on the edge of his makeshift desk. "We wouldn't let our reins be used if they were old and thin. When they start to wear out, we replace them. Why do you want to know?"

He seemed to be a little alarmed, and Nancy guessed he thought she might be an investigator, checking to see if Thurston's was renting unsafe equipment.

"I'm not here to accuse Thurston's of anything," she reassured him. "The fact is, there was an accident yesterday involving one of your sleighs."

"What kind of accident?"

Instead of answering, Nancy said, "Let's say some equipment of yours was damaged, entirely through the negligence of the renters. What would happen? Would they have to pay for what they'd damaged?"

"Sure." Charlie continued to look at her suspiciously. "I'm not sure what you're getting at, but I don't think I should say anything more until Mr. Thurston gets back." His jaw was set in a straight and stubborn line.

I'm not getting anywhere! Nancy thought, frustration building inside her. "Look," she blurted out. "I was in that accident yesterday. As you can see, I'm still in one piece. I don't plan to sue Thurston's, but I do want to know who sawed into a set of your reins yesterday and nearly got me killed!"

Shock played over Charlie's face. "That's terrible!" he said sincerely. "I'm sorry. I guess I'm a little protective of the stables." He paused for a moment. "What was it that you said about the reins?"

"I think someone sabotaged them, but I need to be sure."

Charlie rubbed his jaw and let out a low whistle. "Sabotage— So that's what Mr. Thurston was yelling about yesterday."

"What do you mean?" Nancy asked.

"Well, when Mr. Thurston gets mad, I try to keep out of his way, so I didn't exactly hear everything. But he was going on about some jerk who'd ruined a brand-new set of reins. Mr. Thurston was really burned up about it. The guy didn't get his deposit back."

Nancy leaned forward excitedly. "Do you know who it was?"

Charlie picked up a ledger from the desk and flipped through it until he found the right page, then ran his finger down a column of names. "Here it is. Glover. Matthew Glover."

Nancy drove back toward River Heights, still reeling from what she'd learned. Matt Glover had to have sabotaged her sleigh. Someone had ruined a brand-new set of reins. How many brand-new sets could have been ruined in a day? It had to have been her set, and it *had* to have been Matt. He was the one who had gotten the sleighs from the stable. No one else had gone near them until she, Bess, and George joined him for their ride. He had deliberately tried to hurt her, and that could mean only one thing: Matt was afraid she was going to expose him as a phony. He *was* an impostor, and he had to be working with someone—the person in the red jacket who had spooked her horse.

Nancy braked for a red light. Well, Matt was about to find out she didn't scare so easily! she fumed. The problem was, she still needed concrete proof. She knew the broken reins weren't enough evidence to convince a court that he was an impostor.

When the light turned green, Nancy turned in the direction of the River Heights library. All copies of the local papers for the last ten years were on microfilm there. She intended to check every shred of information about Matt's disappearance five years earlier. Something would come to her. It had to.

Forty-five minutes later Nancy still hadn't found anything that would break the phony Matt's story. Letting out a frustrated sigh, she closed her eyes and massaged them with her fingers. The microfilm was making her headache come back.

Suddenly she felt a strong hand grip her shoulder. Her eyes popped open and she looked up—straight into the blue eyes of Matt Glover.

"Still at it, I see," Matt said. He was using his old teasing voice, but Nancy could hear the undercurrent of steely anger. Or was she just imagining it?

Was it just a coincidence that he was there? Or had he followed her? Suddenly Nancy was glad she was in a public building and not some isolated place. "Still at it," she admitted, trying to act casual.

"Well, you'd better work fast," he said. "By noon tomorrow I'll be granted my rightful place as Clayton Glover's son. The lawyers are drawing up the papers now."

Rightful place! What a bunch of baloney!

Matt gave her his trademark grin, then with a casual wave he sauntered off. Now that Nancy knew for sure he wasn't the real Matt, he seemed smug and arrogant, not charming. He was right about one thing, though. She had to work quickly if she was going to prove he was an impostor before noon the next day!

Nancy returned the microfilm, stepped out into the cold winter air, and briskly walked the short distance to her father's law firm.

"This is a surprise," Carson Drew said, smiling as she came into his office. "Uh-oh. From the dark look on your face, you're not here to tell me I'm the number-one father of the year."

Nancy laughed and gave him a quick hug before taking a seat. "Well, you are, Dad, but I came about something else." She told him what she had figured out about Matt. "He has to be working with someone else, and I have an idea who, but I don't have a shred of proof." She explained about Jake Loomis.

"Well, maybe we can dig something up just by talking. Why don't you talk through what you know about the case and see if we can figure anything out," her father suggested.

"It's worth a try," Nancy agreed. Leaning back in her chair, she began reconstructing her investigation for Carson Drew.

When she got to the part about Tony Giralda, a concerned look came into her father's face. "Nancy, that was privileged information you gave to Tony. Nobody is supposed to know the terms of the will but the lawyers and Matt."

"What?" Nancy leaned forward, beginning to feel excited. "You're sure no one but you and some other lawyers and Matt knew the terms of the will?"

"Positive. Well, there was one other person who knew." He pointed a finger at her, an amused smile on his lips.

Nancy quickly told her father about her visit to Jake Loomis. "The point is," she finished in an excited rush, "when we talked to Loomis, he said he hadn't seen Matt since he was interviewed by him. But he knew all about which businesses would inherit Mr. Glover's money. He *must* have found out from Matt. There's no other way, is there? So they've definitely been in touch."

She remembered seeing Matt on the telephone by the diner that day in Chicago. He might have been speaking to Loomis.

Carson Drew frowned. "This is very serious, Nancy. If Matt told Loomis about the will, that must mean—"

"That we can *prove* he and Matt are partners in a giant scam to steal Mr. Glover's fortune!"

Chapter

Fourteen

NANCY JUMPED UP. "I've got my proof. Loomis and Matt—I mean Gary Page—set up the whole scheme." She gave her father a big hug. "Thanks, Dad. You just helped me clear everything up."

She was already halfway to the door when Carson asked her, "Where are you going?"

"To catch some criminals!" she called over her shoulder.

Her mind was racing as she got back into her Mustang, the pieces of her plan falling together. She had to set a trap to bring Loomis and Matt together, where she could confront them and get hard evidence—evidence to stand up in court. She knew just how to do it, too.

Bess was the answer. There was no way Matt

would let his guard down with Nancy, but he would have no reason to suspect Bess. She had believed in him from the start. As far as Matt was concerned, she was his loyal dupe. Of course, Nancy would first have to convince Bess that Matt was an impostor—something she wasn't looking forward to at all.

First Nancy drove to Tony Giralda's office. After parking in front of his building, she pulled a small notebook and a pen from her purse and carefully composed a short script.

This is Mr. Loomis's client in River Heights. I'm having trouble with my garden, and I need to see Mr. Loomis at seven this evening—in person.

When she was done, she reread it, satisfied. If she could get Tony to call Jake Loomis's office and say exactly that, she was sure it would be enough to set Loomis up.

"You want me to do *what?*" Tony boomed when Nancy proposed her plan to him. He stared at the words.

"You won't be talking to Loomis," she explained. "You'll be speaking to a receptionist. Just give her the message and hang up. There'll be no way he'll ever connect you to the call."

"I don't know. . . ." Tony said.

"Come on, Tony. Where's your sense of justice?"

"Why can't *you* make the call?" he argued.

"It has to be a man's voice, or Loomis will know it wasn't really Matt who called," she told him.

Tony shook his head. "I don't know. I'm not very good at this kind of thing."

"Please, Tony, just practice it a few times. Think of it as a rehearsal for your part in bringing justice to River Heights."

Reluctantly, Tony took the paper and read woodenly. His face was flushed bright red, and he stumbled on every other word.

"Lighten up," Nancy said with a smile. "Try it again."

His second attempt was even worse. Nancy had to struggle to keep from laughing. "You sound like a taped announcement," she said.

"Did I ever say I was an actor?" he retorted irritably.

Nancy read the message out loud, showing him where to pause so that he would sound natural. He got better with each try, and at last Nancy punched out Loomis's number on Tony's phone and handed him the receiver.

Tony clutched it tightly, perspiration beading his forehead and color rising in his cheeks. "I feel like a dope," he said, but then the line was picked up in Chicago. He straightened up and said his piece, then hung up.

"She started to ask questions, so I figured I'd better get off." He let out a huge breath of relief and told her, "I'm shaking all over. Is that what stage fright is like?"

"Not bad, Tony, not bad at all," she said. "You might be headed for a new career."

"Cut it out," he said, but now the pink in his face came from pleasure.

After thanking Tony, Nancy left his office. She braced herself as she drove over to Bess's house. This part of her plan she was dreading.

"Nancy Drew, you're trying to ruin everything!" Bess wailed. "Why can't you just accept that Matt Glover really has come back? Give the guy a break, would you?"

Bess was wearing pink sweats, sitting on the exercise bike in her room.

Nancy sighed and plopped down on Bess's bed. "Come on, Bess. You can't ignore the evidence—"

"That's what you keep telling me," Bess retorted, pedaling furiously, "but I don't see what's so conclusive about it. There's no proof that Matt cut those reins, and you said yourself you weren't sure about his scar. If you want me to go along with some stupid plan to trap him, you can just forget it." She crossed her arms over her chest and said defiantly, "In fact, I think as his *friend* —which you obviously aren't—I should warn him."

"You can't!" Nancy sat up straight on Bess's bed. She *had* to make her understand—and fast.

In an urgent voice Nancy explained again about how Matt must have been the one to tell Loomis which charities were to receive money. "Don't you see? Loomis lied to us when he said he hadn't seen Matt since the interview. That means Loomis and Matt *have* to be working together. It's the only answer.

"And it's not just a matter of the charities who'll be cheated," Nancy continued. "What about Matt, the real Matt? What about his father? It would be an insult to their memories. I'm trying to protect them, too."

Bess still didn't look convinced, but Nancy saw her expression soften a little. "I don't like it," she said dubiously. "What if you're wrong? I'd never be able to forgive myself for being so sneaky. Why do I have to be involved at all?"

"If I could do it, I would, but I can't. Matt doesn't trust me. He wouldn't give me the time of day. He might let down his guard with you, though. Look at it this way, Bess. If he really is Matt Glover, isn't it worth it to prove it beyond any doubt? That way we could all be happy for him."

Bess sighed. "When you put it like that," she said slowly, "it sort of makes sense." She smiled shakily. "What is it I'm supposed to do?"

"I want you to catch him out in a lie, except it won't be a lie he tells. It'll have to be something he says he remembers. Something that never really happened. A lie in reverse."

"What if he says he doesn't remember it?"

"Then I guess we'll know he's the real Matt Glover," Nancy replied. "I'll apologize to you for all my doubts, and everyone will live happily ever after."

Bess grinned. "That's the version I like," she said, "and I'll bet you that's what happens." Her expression grew serious, and Nancy was afraid she might change her mind.

"What's the matter?" Nancy asked.

Bess climbed down from the exercise bike and went over to her closet. "Well, I was just wondering. . . ." She threw open her closet door and started rummaging through her clothes. "What should I wear?"

Nancy grinned. "At least you haven't lost sight of the really important things in life—like the perfect outfit!" She got up from Bess's bed and helped go through her closet. "Whatever you wear should have deep pockets," she said. "I want you to have my tape recorder going, so we'll have proof."

Bess's eyes widened. "That's the kind of thing *you* do," she said.

Nancy pulled out an oversize red sweater with two big patch pockets. "This will be perfect, and you'll look great!"

"Okay." Bess sat down on the edge of her bed and asked, "So what kind of lie do you want me to catch him in?"

"It has to be something from a big event in his

life," Nancy said. "Something he'd remember because of when it happened. *Nobody* could have filled him in on every little detail, it just isn't possible. You know, like his eighteenth birthday, when he got that great sports car— Hey, Loomis had left by then! Hold on, I think I've got it."

She told Bess her plan and then called Mrs. Adams at Glover's Corners. "Are you alone?" she asked. The housekeeper told her that Matt had gone downtown.

Nancy quickly told Mrs. Adams what she had figured out and what she planned to do about it. "Leave the side door open," Nancy instructed after sketching out her scheme. "And when Bess and Matt are safely in the library, come and tell me."

"This isn't going to be dangerous for Bess, is it?" Mrs. Adams sounded concerned.

"No," said Nancy. "Matt won't even know he's been trapped, but we'll have it on tape. By the time I confront Loomis and Matt this evening, Bess will be long gone, and I'll have the police with me. Once they hear the tape, I'm sure the authorities will be eager to take Matt into custody."

The housekeeper promised to let them know the moment Matt returned to the house. When Nancy returned to Bess's room, Bess was wearing the red sweater over a black knit skirt, red stockings, and black boots.

"You look great!" Nancy told her. Seeing

Bess's sad expression, she added softly, "I wouldn't even ask if I didn't think it was very important. I hope I'm wrong, Bess, really I do. But you've got to be prepared for the worst."

Bess nodded shakily.

Nancy had just showed Bess how to use the minirecorder when Mrs. Adams called back and told them that Matt had returned to Glover's Corners.

"This is it," she told Bess, feeling a rush of energy flow through her. "We're on!"

It was late in the afternoon when Nancy eased her Mustang through the gates of the Glover estate. The sun was setting, and the house and grounds were shrouded in dark gray shadows. Nancy was happy for the cover of darkness; Matt would be less likely to see her.

"We'd better park here so he doesn't see my car," she told Bess, stopping just inside the gates. "You can tell him you got dropped off. I'll wait till you're inside, then circle around by the trees to the side door."

Nancy watched as Bess trudged up to the house. As soon as she was inside, Nancy made her way to the side door and flattened herself against the wall so no one could spot her from inside. She checked her watch. Five o'clock.

Twenty minutes later, Mrs. Adams appeared at the side door, opening it soundlessly. "They're in the library now," she whispered. "I'll be in the kitchen."

Nancy slipped inside and tiptoed up the two steps from the side door. Now she was in a hall, with the dining room to her left and the library to the right. The library door wasn't closed, but Nancy was sure she couldn't be seen from this angle.

Once more she flattened herself against the wall just a few feet from the door. If Matt came out for any reason, he would probably use the door that led to the back hall and the kitchen. And if he headed for the door where she was eavesdropping—well, Nancy had to hope that Bess would find some way to warn her so she could duck back to the outside door in time to avoid being seen.

Bess's voice floated out from the library and Nancy heard her leading the conversation to the topic of parties. She said something about having to buy a present for her cousin Louise's birthday party. Nancy grinned—she didn't think Bess even had a cousin named Louise.

"I never seem to be able to choose just the right present," Bess was saying. "When I was a kid I bought some aquarium gravel—you know, the kind that comes in rainbow colors—for a boy who had tropical fish. He started crying when he opened it, and when I asked him what was wrong, he told me all his fish had died the week before."

Matt roared with laughter. "Poor Bess," he said.

Nancy had to suppress her own laughter as she listened to the wild stories Bess was inventing about terrible gifts she had given. She sounded completely natural, and Matt was laughing and egging her on.

"Still," Bess said, her voice dreamy now, "the best party ever was your eighteenth, Matt. It wasn't just that gorgeous car your father gave you, it was—everything!"

"It was a spectacular party," he agreed.

"I was only in junior high back then," Bess went on, "and I remember my friends and I were completely amazed that you invited us. It was the high point of our entire year! I don't think I've ever seen a cake as big as the one you had, not even at weddings."

Nancy caught her breath. This was it.

There had been two cakes, one in the shape of the number one and the other, number eight. Both had been iced in mocha fudge, Matt's favorite at the time.

"Was it your father who thought of having a cake the shape of a giant football, or was it you?" Bess was asking.

"It was me," Matt said, without missing a beat. "I guess I wanted everyone to remember my shining career on the varsity team. Not very modest of me, was it?"

Nancy's breath caught in her throat. He'd fallen for it! Now Bess would know for sure that the guy in there with her *wasn't* Matt Glover.

Nancy knew she had to be devastated by the realization. Now Nancy listened even more attentively, hoping Bess wouldn't give herself away.

"And iced in purple and white," Bess said. Her voice was trembling now, but Matt didn't seem to notice.

"The colors of River Heights High," he said, chuckling.

Nancy silently urged Bess to make some kind of excuse and get out of there. She was sure Bess wouldn't be able to keep up her facade much longer.

Suddenly a loud *crack* rang out from the library. Every muscle in Nancy's body tensed. What was going on? Was Bess in trouble? She heard Matt give a grunt of surprise, then Bess said, "Who's that?" Nancy heard panic in her friend's voice.

A split second later, Bess let out a cry of alarm. Nancy gasped as she heard the sound of something metal clattering onto stone. The flagstone hearth?

The tape recorder! Matt must have found it—and that meant Bess was in danger!

Chapter

Fifteen

Nancy sprang for the doorway, her heart pounding. But just inside the room, she stopped short as her gaze fell on a second man. Jake Loomis!

Nancy realized with dismay that her plan had gotten totally fouled up. Loomis wasn't supposed to arrive for about another hour. But there he was, holding both of Bess's arms behind her in one of his huge hands. In his other hand he held the minirecorder. His face was twisted with fury, and just the sight of it made Nancy shiver.

He glanced at her, his eyes narrowing with recognition. "You!" he spat out. Turning to Matt, he muttered, "She's the one who came snooping around my office. There was another girl with her but not this one." He indicated Bess with his head.

Matt whirled around to face Nancy. "What are you doing here?" he asked.

Ignoring Matt, Nancy said to Jake Loomis, "Let Bess go."

Bess's eyes were wide with fear, and she was trembling. Her arm was twisted painfully behind her, but Loomis didn't release his grip.

"Let her go," Nancy said again, using as firm a voice as she could muster. "What are you afraid of? Do you really have to use all your strength to terrorize someone who's one-third your size?"

Loomis dropped Bess's arms and took a threatening step toward Nancy. "You're a troublemaker," he said. "I should have known—all that nonsense about *Who's Who.*"

"What are you doing here?" Matt directed his curt question to Loomis, biting off each word.

Loomis glared at him. "You should know, you sent me a message to come."

Matt looked surprised. "A message? I didn't send any—" He broke off, staring at Nancy. "She tricked you, Jake."

"Look who's talking about being tricked," Loomis said. "You've let these kids make a fool of you."

"It wasn't easy," Nancy cut in. "He was very good, Mr. Loomis. Almost too good. You have great skills as a coach."

"I don't know what you're talking about,"

Matt said. "Nothing's changed. Bess and I were just talking about parties—nothing heavy—and all of a sudden Jake comes in like a lunatic."

"Come off it," Nancy told him. "You don't think we'll still fall for your charade, do you?"

Unperturbed, Matt turned toward Bess and gave her one of his dazzling smiles. "You believe me, don't you, Bess?"

Nancy watched Bess turn brick red with anger and humiliation. "No, I don't! It so happens, Matt Glover, or whoever you *really* are," Bess fumed, "that your birthday cake was nothing like the one I invented. A cake shaped like a football! A purple and white cake, for the high-school colors? I don't think so."

She gave a scornful laugh, but it turned into a cry of pain as Loomis grabbed her arm and twisted it behind her back again.

"Okay, girls," he said in a cold voice. "I didn't want anything to happen to anyone, but you've brought it on yourselves. You"—he gestured to Nancy—"get over here with your friend. I think we're going for a drive."

Nancy stayed where she was, playing for time. "If Bess and I disappear, don't you think it will make it harder for Matt to claim his legacy? After all, my father *is* the lawyer in question."

"I don't care if your father is the president," Loomis snarled. "Get over here, you little—" He checked himself. "It must have been fun for you to come to my Chicago office and pass yourself off as a researcher for *Who's Who in Business.* You really thought you were putting one over on me."

"Not at all," said Nancy. "I knew right away that you were a smart criminal, even if you are slimy. I'll bet you've always been looking for the chance to pull off this kind of scam."

Loomis smiled. "And my chance came, didn't it? It came in the form of a reporter named Gary Page." He turned toward Matt and said, "The second I saw you, you reminded me so much of Matt Glover I knew my time had come."

"I'm warning you, Jake," Matt barked. "Shut up."

"You're warning *me?"* Loomis laughed. "Who do you think you are? Without me, you'd be nothing, a two-bit hack, a nobody!" He gave Matt a smug look. "I created you, and you're throwing it all away over these—" He threw a look of loathing at Nancy and Bess.

"Stop running your mouth, Jake," Matt said harshly.

As the two men argued, Nancy frantically looked around for a way to escape. There was no way she and Bess were a match for the two men, physically. If they ran, Matt and Loomis were sure to overpower them. She could only hope that Mrs. Adams had heard and called the police —if Loomis hadn't already gotten to her. Nancy shuddered at the thought. For the moment, Nancy decided, all she could do was keep distracting them.

"How did you give yourself that scar on your wrist?" she asked Matt.

Matt glared at her but said nothing.

"Give the girl some credit," Loomis said. "She's on to you."

"And I'm on to *you,* too," she said, turning to Jake Loomis. "It wasn't enough for you to succeed in the landscape gardening business, was it?" she asked Loomis. "When the *Clarion* sent Gary Page to interview you, it seemed like a perfect chance. He looks like Matt would have looked—he's athletic and charming like Matt, and he's even left-handed!"

Loomis shrugged. "Page was a natural. Had a memory like an elephant, too. I knew he could pull off acting like Matt."

Nancy turned to Matt. "Tell me something," she said. "What made you decide to go along with it? Did it take lots of persuasion, or did you agree immediately?"

He glared at her for a moment, before grumbling, "Oh, who cares if we tell you. Where you're going, it won't make any difference." The grin on his face was smug. "It was the money, of course. I'd have been a fool to turn down a chance like this."

"It must have been easy meeting every day," Nancy said. "The *Clarion* is so close to Loomis

Landscaping. You must have been awfully busy, Gary. Working full time as a reporter and then taking lessons from Loomis in your spare time. He must have drawn you a map of Glover's Corners. But you had to memorize all sorts of other details, too. You had to remember to call Mrs. Adams 'Addie,' and to plaster mustard on your sandwiches. You had to learn all the little customs of life at Glover's Corners, like bringing pies and cakes to Mrs. Adams so she wouldn't spend her whole life baking."

Nancy took a deep breath, then pressed on. "You made a terrible mistake with that chocolate cake. You didn't know Mrs. Adams has a violent allergy to chocolate. The real Matt saw her nearly die from eating some by mistake. It's not something he would have forgotten."

Matt grimaced. "I think I can still finesse that one," he said to Loomis.

"It was a class act, Gary," Nancy said, "but you were bound to mess it up. Nobody could have learned all the little details that make up a person's life."

"Like two cakes in the shape of the number 18," Bess piped up.

"I don't see why you're making such a big deal of this." It was Gary Page speaking. "Who would have been hurt? I make a wonderful Matt."

"Oh, brother, I've had enough of this," said Loomis. "Get over here!" he shouted at Nancy.

For emphasis, he twisted Bess's arm viciously, making her shriek again.

Nancy had no choice but to do as he ordered. Her heart was beating hard as she went to stand next to Bess, but she was determined not to show either of the men that she was afraid.

"This is what we're going to do. We're going to drive out into the countryside. It's a deep freeze out there."

Bess started to cry, and Nancy saw that her whole body shook. Ignoring her, Loomis went on in an eerily calm voice. "I'm going to let you out of the car in a field somewhere, twenty miles from any town."

Bess moaned and bit her lip.

"Mother Nature will do the rest," Loomis said. "I won't have to lay a hand on either of you."

"No one will believe we died by accident," Nancy said. "They'll connect it to Gary, and he won't go down without taking you. You played your game, and you lost. Why not just admit it?"

"I'm not a loser, kid." Loomis sneered.

"Wait a minute," Gary cut in. "Maybe we can talk this over. If you girls could keep a secret, we still have a way out of this. There might even be some money in it for you. I'd be willing to share—there's more than enough to go around."

He looked beseechingly at Bess and shot her that same flirtatious look, but she just glared at him.

"Shut up," Loomis said harshly. "If you think these girls could keep a secret, you're crazier than I thought." He shoved Nancy. "Let's get going," he said, "and don't bother to scream. Nobody will hear you. I've already tied up your gray-haired friend in the kitchen. She'll have to go with you girls, of course.

"Now move it!"

Before she could do anything, Nancy heard a crashing noise come from the hallway.

"What the—?" Loomis turned toward the doorway as the crashing noises came closer. Suddenly his face went slack with shock.

Following his gaze, Nancy saw two enormous dogs come hurtling into the room, growling and baring their huge teeth. Grabbing Bess's arm, Nancy tore her friend away from Loomis just as the dogs made a flying leap toward them.

Chapter

Sixteen

Nancy and Bess barely managed to jump out of the dogs' way. Loomis, too, leapt back, but the enormous dogs kept after him, cornering him on the couch.

Nancy had recognized Tony Giralda's dogs, Fred and Max, at once. Her experience with the dogs had shown her that they weren't fierce, but Loomis didn't know that. He had scrambled over the sofa and was cowering against the wall in panic.

That took care of one criminal, she thought, but there was still one more.

Nancy spun around and looked for Gary, who was edging away from the group. Seeing her, he took off at a run toward the rear door, the one Loomis must have used to get in unseen by

Nancy. Nancy sprinted after him, catching up to him just before he reached the doorway and immobilizing him with a quick judo kick to his side. Gary let out a groan as he fell and lay curled up on the floor, clutching his ribs.

"Way to go, Nancy!" a deep voice called out behind her.

Turning, she saw that Tony Giralda had come into the library. Mrs. Adams was there, too, and she and Bess were standing close together on the opposite side of the room from Fred, Max, and Loomis. They seemed to be as frightened as Loomis was of the big dogs, who were now standing with their paws up on the sofa and growling deep in their throats.

"Hello there, Mr. Loomis, glad you could be here," Tony said, going over to the sofa.

"Someone should call the police," Nancy said.

"Over my dead body," Loomis said, but his voice was shaky.

"That can be arranged," Tony told him. "Fang and Claw here are trained attack dogs. I have only to say the word and they'll tear you to shreds." Nancy had to suppress a laugh at the aliases Tony had given Fred and Max. "I called the police as soon as I found Mrs. Adams tied up in the kitchen."

Nancy saw that Gary was getting to his feet, still clutching his side, and she gestured for him to walk over and stand by the couch, where Fred and Max could keep an eye on him, too.

Fred was still making that deep, menacing sound in his throat, and Nancy hoped he wouldn't stop—at least until the police showed up.

Holding out her hand, Nancy spoke to Loomis in a firm voice. "I'd like my tape recorder back, please. Hand it over to me very carefully. We don't want to alarm Fang."

Loomis held the minirecorder out and tossed it on the couch. "It won't do you much good," he scoffed. "It hit those flagstones pretty hard before. The thing's probably broken."

"I wouldn't be so sure," Nancy said, picking it up. She rewound the tape a little and then hit the Play button. Bess's voice came into the room, loud and clear. "Was it your father who thought of having a cake the shape of a giant football, or was it you?"

Behind Nancy, Bess giggled nervously at the sound of her own voice.

"That doesn't prove anything," Gary said. "Who remembers a cake from years ago? You'd be laughed out of court with that evidence."

"Maybe you've forgotten all the things you just confessed when you thought it didn't matter, since you planned on leaving us to die in the snow," Nancy pointed out.

"*I* haven't forgotten," Bess called from behind Nancy.

"We'll both testify to everything in court," Nancy said. "You two are going to jail for a long time."

Loomis's face had turned a deep purple color. With a cry of rage, he lunged at Nancy, hands raised, but she ducked aside easily. Loomis crouched, ready to spring at her, but he hesitated as the high-pitched whine of a siren filtered into the room.

A moment later two squad cars with flashing red lights raced up the drive and screeched to a halt in front of the house.

"The police!" Mrs. Adams exclaimed. "And not a moment too soon."

"Well, it's been quite an evening!" Mrs. Adams said. She, Nancy, Bess, and Tony sat around the kitchen table. None of them had wanted to remain in the library after the police took Gary Page and Jake Loomis away.

"We're lucky it ended the way it did," Nancy said, taking a sip of her cider. Mrs. Adams had made a big pot of it, and now the scent of cloves and cinnamon filled the air.

"It wasn't all luck, dear," Mrs. Adams reminded her. "The police were delighted that you had that tape.

"I'm just glad it's over. I thought I would drop dead of fear when I saw those beasts," the housekeeper added, chuckling. "I thought they were the most fearsome-looking attack dogs I'd ever seen."

"That makes two of us," Bess said. "Who would have known they were such sweethearts?"

Nancy glanced affectionately at the big dogs, who were lying contentedly at Tony's feet, chomping on pieces of beef bone that Mrs. Adams had put in soup bowls for them.

"They deserve that reward for coming to the rescue," she said. "Which reminds me, how did you know to come here, Tony?"

"I started thinking of that phone call you had me make," he began, reaching down to pet Max. "The more I thought about it, the more dangerous I thought the situation was. I went to your house to warn you, but your housekeeper said you weren't home. That's when I got a pretty good idea of where you were, and I drove out here. I saw your car parked down at the end of the drive, and I had a feeling—"

"A gut feeling?" Nancy asked, grinning.

"Right, a feeling you were in danger. I parked down by your car, then came up to the house by foot. I saw through the window what was going on. Luckily the side door was open. Anyway, when I got inside, I found Mrs. Adams tied up in the kitchen." He held up his hands and smiled. "The rest is history."

"But how did you get Fred and Max to act so threatening?" Bess asked, a puzzled look on her face.

Tony reached down again to pat the big dogs, who had finished chewing on their bones and were sleeping with their muzzles resting on their huge front paws. "There's one thing that drives

Fred and Max crazy. They can't stand getting a bath, and always put up a big fight."

"So you dumped some water on them, and presto—enter Fred and Max, barking ferociously," Nancy guessed. "I was wondering why the fur around their heads was wet."

"I didn't like doing it," said Tony, "but I figured it would be the best way to stall until the police showed up. By the way, who locked you in my office with Fred and Max the night we went skating?"

"It had to be Gary, since Jake wasn't around then. He must have followed me to see what I was up to," Nancy replied.

"I want to thank you for everything, Tony," Bess said. "If it weren't for you, Nancy and I might have ended up as icicles a hundred miles from anywhere."

"My mistake was in thinking that Loomis wouldn't get here until later," Nancy said. "Tony told him seven o'clock in our phone call, but he obviously decided not to wait until then. In fact, I think he was already here. I bet he never left the area after causing our sleigh accident yesterday."

Bess's blue eyes went wide. "You mean he's been here all along?" she asked.

"Not here at Glover's Corners, but close by. There are lots of motels around."

"He must have called his office for his messages," said Tony, "and the receptionist said that stuff about his client in River Heights having trouble with his garden."

"And now his car's out in *our* garden," Mrs. Adams said. "I do hope the police will take it away."

Bess looked at the housekeeper and asked, "Where will you go, Mrs. Adams? When all this is over, I mean."

"I imagine I'll go to Florida," Mrs. Adams told her. "I have a sister there, you know. Besides, the winters here are beginning to get to me. Old bones don't like the cold as much as young ones do.

"Still," Mrs. Adams went on, on a dreamier note, "it was lovely, having you all here again. I suppose I was fooling myself to think we could bring the old days back."

"But it *was* like the old days," Bess insisted.

"No, dear," corrected Mrs. Adams, "it only seemed like them. In the old days that handsome young man who skated with you had a good heart. Matt was a wonderful person, just like his father. The man out on the pond this time was wicked, through and through."

She turned shining eyes on Nancy, Bess, and Tony. "But thanks to you, he'll get what he deserves."

"You bet," said Bess, grinning. "He might have been hoping for ten to twenty million, but now he'll get ten to twenty years!"

Chapter

Seventeen

W ELL," SAID TONY, scraping his chair back, "I have to get back to my office."

"We should go, too," Nancy said to Bess. "I'd like to go to my house and tell my dad the case is over. We could stop by to pick up George on the way."

Nancy, Bess, and Tony hugged Mrs. Adams, then trudged down the long drive to their cars.

"Nancy?" Bess asked after Tony had driven off. Nancy saw that there was a wistful look in her friend's eyes. "Weren't you ever taken in by Matt—I mean, Gary Page? Not even for the tiniest minute?"

"Sure," Nancy answered. "Especially when we were out on the pond, in the moonlight, and we were having so much fun. I was just as fooled as anyone."

Bess sighed.

"Don't feel bad, Bess. You really wanted it to be true that Matt was alive. And Gary Page put on a really convincing act. He was charming, handsome, generous—he said and did everything exactly right. No one could ever blame you for believing in him."

Bess smiled sadly. "When he fell for that lie about the cake, *I* was the one who felt like a fool at first. I mean, I actually thought I could fall in love with that guy! But then I just got madder and madder at him for being so deceitful." She shook her head. "What a jerk."

Nancy gave Bess a warm smile. She knew Bess must feel sad that Matt had turned out to be a fake, but at least she was mad at him, too.

Nancy and Bess climbed into the Mustang and went to pick up George. As the three girls then drove toward the Drews', Nancy and Bess told George what had happened out at Glover's Corners.

"You're kidding!" George exclaimed. "I can't believe I missed the wrap-up of the whole case!"

"I wouldn't have minded missing it a bit," said Bess. "It was pretty scary."

"It was even scarier if you knew Fred and Max's true nature," Nancy added with a laugh. "I was afraid they'd start wagging their tails and making friends with those goons."

The lights were on at the Drews' house, and Carson Drew greeted the girls with a big smile as they came in the front door.

"The police chief just called and told me what happened," he said. "He said to tell you that Jake Loomis and Gary Page both gave signed confessions." Carson smiled proudly at his daughter. "The police have an open-and-shut case. Page and Loomis will be going to jail, I can promise you that."

"Great!" Nancy said. She and Bess sat on the den sofa, while George settled herself in an easy chair.

"By the way," Carson went on, "that was clever of you to have Tony Giralda's guard dogs to protect you. Otherwise you would have been in great danger."

The three girls looked at one another, then dissolved in laughter, leaving Carson to stare at them and shake his head.

"There's one thing I don't understand," Bess said, still giggling a little. "How could Gary Page have aced that lie-detector test?"

"I don't understand it either," Nancy put in. "I know they're not completely reliable, but how could he have done so well? And what made him so eager to take it, when he knew he was lying?"

"I have a theory about it," Mr. Drew said. "The conspiracy to commit fraud between Gary Page and Jake Loomis was no small thing. It was planned on a grand scale. If it succeeded, they would split a huge fortune.

"They were smart enough to know they couldn't carry it off without a lot of preparation. In a sense, Gary went into training as an athlete would."

"He went into training to *become* Matt," Nancy said, nodding. "That makes sense."

"Yes," her father continued. "To become Matt. Not to imitate him perfectly, but to *be* Matthew Glover for the rest of his life. He submerged himself in so much detail, he worked so hard at being Matt, I think in the end he might really have believed he *was* Matt."

"Then why did the test indicate he was lying about having been in Colorado?" Nancy asked.

"It turns out he never had been in Colorado. He's from Nebraska. He did work on a paper in Iowa City, but he's never been west of Omaha."

"Why should that make any difference?" George wanted to know. "He lied about everything else easily enough. Why couldn't he lie about being in Colorado?"

"I think I know," Nancy said. "Colorado, the accident itself, wasn't a part of his training with Loomis. Why should it have been? He'd had amnesia, and even if he snapped out of it when he saw his father's obituary, he might not remember the actual accident, anyway."

"Yes, I think you're right, Nancy," Carson Drew said.

"In other words," said George, "he couldn't believe in anything Loomis hadn't prepared him for."

"Well put, George," said Nancy's father. "Think of Loomis as the trainer and Gary Page as a racehorse."

"A racehorse that finally tripped on a hurdle," said Nancy.

There was a giggle from Bess before she put in, "A hurdle shaped like a football and iced in white and purple."

At that moment the phone rang. Nancy went to answer it.

"Hi, Nan," came Ned's voice. "Sorry to call so late, but no one was at your place all day except Hannah."

Nancy felt a familiar warm tingle at the sound of his voice. "It was one of those days," she told him.

"One of what days? What happened?" he asked. "You sound a little tired."

There was so much to explain. "It's a long story," she said into the phone. "And I've got company. I'll call you back and tell you everything as soon as Bess and George leave, okay?"

She talked with him a few more minutes, then said goodbye and hung up. When she returned to the living room, Bess and George were eating chocolate-chip cookies from a plate on the low table in front of the sofa.

"Solving cases with Nancy always makes me so hungry," Bess said, biting into one of the chewy cookies.

Nancy was reaching for a cookie herself when her father commented, "I'm sure there'll be some interesting reading in the papers tomorrow."

Bess sat up on the sofa. "About how we caught the criminals?"

"No," Carson replied. "About Mr. Glover's will. Now that nobody's contesting it, the information can be published."

"Since the ban of secrecy has been lifted," Nancy said to her father, "can you tell us who's going to get all that money?"

Carson Drew pulled a sheet of paper from his jacket pocket and unfolded it. "As a matter of fact, I have a copy of the press release that's going to the media." He began to read aloud.

" 'The will of Clayton Glover leaves his magnificent residence, Glover's Corners, to the town of River Heights. It is to be used as a historical museum and gathering place for citizens of the community. In an unusual move, Glover's will dictates that the grounds of his estate be turned into a park and that the pond be used for ice skating in season.' "

"Way to go, Mr. Glover," George said, clapping her hands.

Carson glanced at the girls and smiled. " 'The entire complex will be called the Matthew Glover

Park,' " he went on, " 'in memory of Mr. Glover's son, who was killed five years ago on a skiing holiday in Colorado.' "

Carson then skimmed over the names of the local charities who would receive money. As Nancy had known, Giralda's Environmental Action was on the list.

"Great," said Nancy when her father told them the annual sum Tony would receive. "Now he'll be able to expand and get the help he deserves."

"Let's hear it for Fred and Max!" George shouted.

"What about Mrs. Adams?" Bess asked.

"A trust fund is to be set up for her," Carson assured the girls. "Mr. Glover mentioned special thanks to her for her faithful service. The press release also mentions Matt." He read again from the paper. " 'None of these bequests would have been possible if Mr. Glover's son, who would be twenty-three, had lived. We can only speculate as to how Matthew Glover would have used the vast wealth his father would have left to him.' "

Carson refolded the paper and looked up. "That's it."

A deep silence followed. Nancy looked at Bess, who wore a thoughtful expression. Nancy hoped hearing about Matt hadn't upset her too much.

"Well," Bess said at last, "something good came out of all this."

"Definitely," George agreed. "Mr. Glover

made it possible for the good old days to go on forever."

Bess shook her head. "That's not what I meant, although it's certainly a good thing."

"What *did* you mean, Bess?" Nancy asked.

"The real Matt Glover might still be wandering around with amnesia," Bess said. Grinning, she reached for another chocolate-chip cookie. "He could still come home."

George rolled her eyes in disbelief, but Nancy reached out and hugged Bess. "You know what?" she said. "You're probably right."

Nancy's next case:

George's neighbor Mark Rubin has been canned by his detective agency. J. Christopher Johnson, subject of an embezzlement investigation, has vanished in a helicopter crash—and Mark's boss blames him for blowing the case. But Mark is convinced that with Nancy's help he can blow the case wide open. He claims Johnson is still alive!

Was the crash an accident? Was it murder? Or was it all a masquerade? Nancy's getting close to the truth—maybe too close for comfort. The mystery of Christopher Johnson's fate has become a question of life or death . . . for Nancy Drew . . . in *INTO THIN AIR*, Case #57 in The Nancy Drew Files™.